Donald Fraser

Metaphors in the Gospels

Donald Fraser

Metaphors in the Gospels

ISBN/EAN: 9783742811370

Manufactured in Europe, USA, Canada, Australia, Japa

Cover: Foto ©Andreas Hilbeck / pixelio.de

Manufactured and distributed by brebook publishing software
(www.brebook.com)

Donald Fraser

Metaphors in the Gospels

METAPHORS IN THE GOSPELS.

A SERIES OF SHORT STUDIES.

BY

DONALD FRASER, D.D.

AUTHOR OF
"SYNOPTICAL LECTURES ON THE BOOKS OF HOLY SCRIPTURE."
"THE SPEECHES OF THE HOLY APOSTLES," ETC.

NEW YORK:
ROBERT CARTER & BROTHERS,
530 BROADWAY.
1885.

CONTENTS.

CONTENTS.

PREFACE.

Books on the Parables of Christ are many; but we do not know of even one devoted to the exposition of those similitudes, so frequent in the oral teaching of our Saviour, which do not take the narrative form or reach the dimensions of a parable. Benjamin Keach's "Key to Open Scripture Metaphors" is much more than a key. Going over the whole field of Scripture, it takes up every figure of speech, and draws out lists of parallels, disparities, and inferences on each, with a pious, though sometimes almost grotesque, ingenuity. Not so much the age as the size and plan of this work have made it obsolete. "The Lesser Parables of our Lord," by the late Rev. William Arnot, seemed to promise just what we wanted; but the volume so entitled turns out to be a posthumous compilation of sermons, beginning indeed with lesser parables, but of these treating only five. Professor A. B. Bruce furnishes a few valuable pages on what he calls Parable-germs in his work on the " Parabolic Teaching of Christ."   But no writer, so far as known to us, has yet attempted to deal with these in any sort of complete fashion; and therefore we hope that our studies will not be regarded as a superfluous addition to expository literature.

We have not included in our plan all the metaphors which occur in the four evangelical narratives, but confined ourselves to those which were employed by Jesus Christ.   Accordingly, our list does not include " the axe at the root of the tree," " the fan and threshing-floor," or " the Lamb of God," all of which phrases are attributed to John the Baptist.

The term " metaphor " we adopt, without any pretence of strict accuracy, simply as the most convenient to cover all the tropes and similitudes which our Lord employed to illustrate and enforce His meaning.   We do not trouble ourselves about the grammatical and rhetorical distinction of metonymy, metaphor, synecdoche, and allegory.   Of those similitudes and comparisons which are on our list, that of the Two Builders may almost rank as a parable; those of the True Bread and the True Vine may be styled allegories ; while that of the Shepherd is called by St. John a Παροιμία; and Christ Himself describes many of His sayings to the disciples by this last word.   The Revised

Version translates the word as "parable" in the 10th chapter of St. John's Gospel, putting "proverb" in the margin; and in the 16th chapter of the same book gives "proverbs" in the text and places "parables" in the margin. In this inconsistency it follows the Authorised Version; but in truth, neither parable nor proverb is a good rendering. The *parœmia*, as Meyer correctly explains, may mean "any species of expression that deviates from the common course (*oimos*)." We prefer to use the title "Metaphors in the Gospels," because in all the sayings of Christ treated of in this volume the element of analogy and comparison will be found.

The Great Prophet dealt largely in illustration because He spoke to "the common people," who in every country, but especially in the East, must be helped in this way to apprehend generalised truth. Sometimes He gave an enigmatical turn to His speech in order to stimulate thought in His disciples, and at the same time to baffle those bystanders who were anxious to cavil and condemn. He never introduced a metaphor for the mere purpose of decorating His public addresses or gratifying a poetic fancy. Some of His illustrations, as well as of His parables, are pathetic and beautiful; but generally they are very realistic, and are addressed quite as much to reason and common sense as to imagination.

Every religious teacher must use metaphors, and the higher the religion the greater the need of them. The objects and interests spoken of are too great and holy to be adequately contained in didactic and logical forms. They require type, allegory, parable, word-picture, and suggestive simile in order to reach the human understanding and heart. And of this method of conveying and illuminating religious truth Jesus of Nazareth was the most perfect Master that the world has seen. How naturally His metaphors rose out of the occasion, and appealed to the observation and experience of those who heard Him, we have tried to show again and again in the following pages.

It may be proper to mention at the outset that our quotations from the New Testament are almost invariably taken from the Revised Version.

METAPHORS IN THE GOSPELS.

I.

SALT.

"Ye are the salt of the earth: but if the salt have lost its savour, wherewith shall it be salted? it is henceforth good for nothing, but to be cast out and trodden under foot of men."— ST. MATT. v. 13.

"Salt therefore is good: but if even the salt have lost its savour, wherewith shall it be seasoned? It is fit neither for the land nor for the dunghill: men cast it out."—ST. LUKE xiv. 34, 35.

IT is a mark of genius to see in common things what is not commonplace, and to make familiar words and objects luminous with meaning. Jesus of Nazareth had this power in a quite exceptional degree; yet one feels that the term "genius" does not quite suit Him, does not adequately express the calm penetration of His mind. What we recognise in Him is a consummate wisdom, piercing in its insight, serene in its temper,

A

powerful in its utterance. As made known to us in the Gospels, He is at once the most profound and the least technical of all religious teachers. He saw the heart of men and things, and drew hidden facts and truths to light; but even in touching the most difficult matters, used no recondite term or phrase of subtlety. Enough for Him the language of everyday life and the popular proverbs of the time, with such illustrations as the houses, gardens, and fields of Palestine supplied. Of them, indeed, He made such apt and copious use, that one who has read the Gospels carefully cannot see bread, water, wine, oil, or salt, cannot look at the grass, the fruit trees, or the birds of the air, cannot so much as feel the wind play upon his cheek, without a suggestion of truth taught and emphasised by the Lord Christ.

The first metaphor which occurs in St. Matthew's report of our Saviour's words is a very homely one.

Common salt is valued for its antiseptic quality. A little fine salt is agreeable to the taste; but the point of the illustration rests on the power of salt, coarse or fine, to preserve animal tissues from decay. Christ described His disciples as salt of the earth or of the land. They were not men of much refinement, but they had in them the saline property which would make them morally and spiritually useful to all around.

This substance was taken by the ancients as an emblem of wit and piquant wisdom; but our Lord gave it a larger and deeper meaning. He had described in the Beatitudes the features and elements of that character which should be formed by His disciples, and would make them useful to other men. It was a type of character which He alone was competent to describe, and which He alone has perfectly exemplified. If we may speak of it as of a tree, its root is in the soil of meekness and humility, watered by godly sorrow. Its strong stem is the desire of righteousness, and its fruits are mercifulness, purity of heart, and the love of peace. The Master warned His disciples that possession of such a character would not gain for them the world's favour.

On the contrary, it would provoke persecution and reproach. But such as had this salt in themselves could never be without a beneficial influence on the society around them. Wherever they might dwell, they would be the salt of the land.

The Latin Church, in its materialistic fashion, employs actual salt in the baptismal service. The priest puts it into the mouth of the person, adult or infant, who is baptized.* It is an unauthorised ceremony; but it is a sort of traditional witness to the obligation lying on all Christians to have in themselves that which salt might symbolise. Our Lord requires that all who follow Him shall have that style of character which savours of the kingdom of heaven, and so exert a morally antiseptic influence on others.

Noah, as a just man, was salt in the old

---

* "Quum sal in illius os, qui ad baptismum adducendus est, inseritur, hoc significari perspicuum est, eum fidei doctrina et gratiæ dono consecuturum esse ut a peccatorum putridine liberetur, saporemque bonorum operum percipiat, et divinæ sapientiæ pabulo dilectetur."—*Cat. Conc. Trid.*, q. 65.

world, but he was not enough to save mankind when "all flesh had corrupted his way upon the earth." Lot was as salt among the dwellers in Sodom, when "in seeing and hearing he vexed his righteous soul from day to day with their lawless deeds;" but it was more than he could do to stay that terrible corruption. Ten righteous men might have saved the city, but not one. The Lord Jesus, purposing to effect a vast and permanent moral change, not only in the land of Judea, but in the corrupt Gentile world, set Himself to provide a sufficient quantity of salt. He would not send forth a multitude of ill-trained adherents. More good was to be done by a much smaller number of disciples well prepared and thoroughly imbued with His Spirit; and yet not too few. They must be numerous enough not to be crushed into obscurity; and they must teach and train others to join them, and to succeed them as the saviours of society and the salt of many lands.

A candid view of the influence of Christianity on that wicked world into which Apostles and Evangelists pushed their way, and in which the primitive Churches were planted, must lead any one to the conclusion that a species of moral " salt " was then applied to a society otherwise hastening to decay ; and it is important to remember that this influence was exerted not by the diffusion of a literature, or by the performance of prodigies, or by the hand of authority, but simply by the individual and social life of men and women—a few of high degree, but far more in humble station, and not a few of them slaves—who had some new element of wisdom and goodness in their minds and hearts—who, in fact, had salt in themselves.

If there is much ineffective Christianity in the present age, it is due to the lack of salt. Christian literature has become immense in bulk, and sermons are innumerable, but these cannot of themselves subdue the corruption which is in the world. Signs and wonders, even if we could command them, would not suit the case. The hand of authority cannot produce conviction or faith ; and no one thinks of invoking it. What the world needs is the influence, passive and active, of Christian men and women, who have grown into "the Beatitudes," and therefore must be salt of the land whereon they dwell; must be felt, and felt for good.

One may often meet with a man who avows himself quite incredulous of miracles and very sceptical about certain parts of the Bible, and yet admits that the moral effect produced by Christianity on the ancient Roman world says much for its Divine origin. But he not unreasonably asks that a similar moral energy should be exhibited now. And here lies the weakness of much of our modern argumentation on the evidences of Christianity. It is not sufficiently sustained by those who profess and call themselves Christians. So far as scholarship and dialectic skill can prove our faith Divine, we are exceedingly well served. But we want more proof in deeds as well as words. The multitudes in Christendom who are doubtful or indifferent need to see the true Christians who are among them living to better purpose, and to feel by daily contact with them that they have "salt in themselves."

To be salt of the land, then, is to be in the highest sense useful to our fellow-men.

I. *Usefulness is a duty.*

It is the end which the Lord has in view in calling us to be His disciples. He teaches us that we may teach others; blesses us that we may bless others.

This method may be traced through all history. Israel received a holy calling as a nation, not for its own sake, but in order to be as salt among the nations of the earth, maintaining a witness for the true God and His law of righteousness. Then within that chosen nation prophets and holy men were especially taught and favoured in order that they might be as salt to their own country-men, and preserve them from apostasy. On the same principle the Church was made as salt to the world, and the pious in the Church as salt to the Christian community itself, to save it from decay.

Long and severe was the struggle between the Christian salt and the corruption of the Roman world, and many grew weary of the process and withdrew. They fled to the deserts and to lonely caves in order to save their own souls, as they supposed, and to preserve their piety in seclusion. Thus arose the Cenobite and monastic system, which committed the error of separating the salt from the substance which it was meant to cure, ultimately setting up "religious houses" with closed doors and barred windows, instead of religious households in the midst of society, shedding a bright and healthy influence on every side. The result of this mistake was that the earth again became corrupt, and the salt itself lost much of its strength and savour.

Protestantism has abolished monastic establishments, but it has, as yet, failed to impress Christian people, in anything like a sufficient degree, with the obligation of usefulness, or to train them for the discharge of such an obligation. All that seems to be thought needful by many a Protestant Christian is to secure the salvation of his own soul, to ascribe this boon to the grace of God, and to contribute some money for the support of preachers and missionaries that they may do good. There is no sufficient persuasion of the grand fact that all who are blessed in Christ are intended to bless others ; that all His disciples, in private as well as official life, are seasoned with salt in order that they may exert a wholesome influence on all whom they reach in daily, or even in occasional intercourse.

II. *The great secret of usefulness is goodness.*

It is a favourite saying that "knowledge is power;" and in many directions it is true. But when we refer to the energy which diffuses moral health and resists corruption, the better aphorism is that "goodness is power." He is a benefactor of his kind who does righteousness, shows mercy, and makes peace.

Not a word here of ritual. Jesus Christ laid no stress on ceremonial, and made no allusion to mystic prerogatives to be vested in a priestly order. He simply taught that His followers, as subjects of the kingdom of heaven, ought to have a righteousness exceeding that which was vaunted by the Scribes and Pharisees. He enumerated the chief properties of a Christian character or soul of goodness, and proclaimed that all who through grace acquire such a character are the salt of the earth and the light of the world. The emphasis is laid not on saying, or even on doing, but on being. The first rule for Christian usefulness is to be out and out a good Christian. It is possible for one to talk admirably yet fail to persuade, and to do many things about the Church and charitable institutions, or, as the modern fashion is, sit on many committees, and yet accomplish very little good, because his own spiritual life is weak and uncertain. He has not enough of salt in himself, and nothing can compensate for the deficiency in that pungent element. But, on the other hand, the way of usefulness lies open to every man, woman, or child that acquires, by the operation of the Holy Spirit, that type of intrinsic character which our Lord delineated in the seven Beatitudes. Such salt is good, and he who has it cannot pass through life useless or insignificant.

III. *The faculty for usefulness may decay.*
Our Saviour warned the disciples against losing the savour of salt.

Those who heard Him could be at no loss to understand the phrase. They were aware that the salt of Syria, when long exposed to sun and air and rain, became quite insipid. Various travellers have reported on this in modern times. And such spoilt salt is good for nothing. It must not be thrown on land, for it would blight its fertility. Nothing can be done with it, but to lay it as a sort of rough gravel on the roads, where it is trodden under foot. So useless are those Christians who lose the savour of goodness and wisdom from on high, having a form of godliness without the power.

For Churches, relapse is no imaginary danger. History tells too sad a tale to the contrary. What did Christ-refusing Judaism become on the earth but salt without savour, which the stern besom of the Roman army swept out into the street or world's thoroughfare to be trodden down? What was the future of those congregations, formed of Jews and Gentiles, which are addressed in the Epistles of St. Paul, and those in the province of Asia to which seven messages are directed in the

Book of Revelation? They lost their savour by admitting corruptions of faith and life, and letting their first love wane; so that they were rejected, and some of them were swept out by the ruthless besom of the Moslem, as so much spoilt, insipid salt. Three hundred years ago, the Reformed Churches were a wholesome and pungent salt in the West, but in nearly all of them defection followed. Some have tended to unbelief, others to superstition, and in these the power of goodness has decayed. It is a question whether they retain enough, or can regain enough, of savour through God's mercy to fulfil the chief end of their existence, or whether other and more faithful Churches must be formed to save the nations from the ungodliness, selfishness, secularism, and anarchy which seriously threaten them.

The danger which is so evident on the large scale is a real one for individual Christians too. These may bless a whole community by their quiet influence and unobtrusive example of virtue in the fear of God. But, alas! if their salt lose its saltness! And what is this but that men once wise grow foolish; once devout, grow negligent of prayer; once zealous, grow lukewarm; once generous, grow stingy; once humble, grow vain; once gentle, grow harsh and arrogant? Can any one say that such declension never occurs? And if the case does occur, what can be more useless than such a Christian? He is less profitable to God and man than the most raw and ignorant beginner, who, if he blunder ever so much, is at all events fresh and sincere. And for the unfaithful disciple himself, how dark the prospect! Backsliding, it is true, may be healed, and a heart that has cooled towards Christ may be warmed again; but, while a sudden fall under strong temptation is often promptly remedied by Divine grace to the penitent, nothing is more difficult than the permanent recovery of those who have gradually and wilfully fallen away and lost savour. We do not say that even this is impossible with God; but it is so precarious a thing that every one should beware of the first symptoms of moral and spiritual declension, lest they bring him to shame, as so much spoilt salt, fit for nothing but to be trodden under foot.

We may depend on it that the Lord would not have spoken superfluous warnings. A wise disciple, hearing the caution against salt losing its savour, will not cry, " No fear of this ever being true of me!" but rather ask softly, " Lord, is it I?" He will not assert, " I shall never fail in my Christian love and earnestness!" but rather make his lowly request, " Grant, Lord, I never may!"

II.

LIGHT.

"Ye are the light of the world. A city set on a hill cannot be hid. Neither do men light a lamp, and put it under the bushel, but on the stand ; and it shineth unto all that are in the house. Even so let your light shine before men, that they may see your good works, and glorify your Father which is in heaven."
—St. Matt. v. 14-16.

"Again therefore Jesus spake unto them, saying, I am the light of the world : he that followeth me shall not walk in the darkness, but shall have the light of life."—St. John viii. 12.

THAT the followers of Christ are "the salt of the earth" suggests intrinsic qualities of wisdom and goodness. That they are "the light of the world" suggests their extrinsic bearing and conduct. The reference is to the openness and visibility of their religious life.

It may be a question how far the human mind of Jesus Christ was aware of the extent of the world. There is no doubt that His hearers had a very inadequate conception of its size and population. But the Spirit of

wisdom whereby all His words were guided
had no such limitation; and such expressions
as "light of the world," "God so loved the
world," were expressly intended to lead forth
the disciples into wide fields of thought and
sympathy, and to prepare the Church for a
range of usefulness far beyond what it had
entered into the minds of Jews or Galileans
to conceive.

I. *Jesus Christ, the Light of the World.*

It was in sore need of light when He came.
The sages and moralists of the most advanced
nations had not so much lit up the world
as sent out sparks which made its darkness
visible. In Judea lamps had been lit from
heaven, but they were growing very dim.
Fed with unholy oil by Pharisees and Sadducees, they were going out. In contrast
with these, John the Baptist was a lamp that
burned and shone. Yet he was not the light
of life, but only a herald and a witness.
When Jesus appeared the True Light shone.
Now "that which makes manifest is light;"
and so Jesus Christ discovered to mankind

moral truths and objects of which the world was ignorant or regardless. He revealed with a heavenly power of demonstration the fatherhood of God, the bitter fountain of sin in the human heart, the freeness of grace, the beauty of humility, and the righteousness of the kingdom of heaven.

Into the consideration of such a metaphor as this we are not to import those conceptions of the nature and laws of light which recent scientific discoveries have supplied. Our Lord spoke to the men of His own time and country so that they might understand Him, using popular language in a popular sense. Enough that the sun is to mankind the grand source and centre of light. So is Jesus Christ no mere lamp, as an ordinary sage or prophet might be, but the sun, the source and centre of that light of life and truth which is being diffused wherever Christ is known and Christians dwell.

II. *Christians the light of the world.*

This is because Christ lives in them, and "the life is the light of men." It is because they learn of Him, derive from Him, and reflect His way of thought and feeling.

This expression -has been illustrated by reference to the face of Moses, which shone after his converse with Jehovah, or to the reflection of light from burnished mirrors flashing in the sun. But the reference made by our Lord to the house-lamps, so familiar to all His audience, yields a better and simpler explanation. Only it must be borne in mind that the fire is caught from a heavenly fire, the light from a heavenly light. And then the lamp sheds its quiet lustre on all that are in the house—*i.e.*, the Christian shows something of Christ to the family and social circle around.

He must do so. When the lamp is lit, it must shine. When a city is set on a hill, it has no option as to visibility. Christians are under a sort of moral compulsion to shine as lights in the world. Yet it is necessary to have the conscience exercised and the will directed by the Lord's command. Let your light shine.

In every, even the poorest, house in Galilee,

a lamp was set on a stand which rested on the floor, and was lit when the sun went down. It sufficed for all the household. There was also in every house a corn measure, called in the English New Testament "the bushel," though it was in size nearer an English peck. Every one therefore caught the idea when Jesus pointed out how perverse and absurd it would be to set the lamp under the corn measure. Its place was on the stand.

And such is the place assigned by God to the disciples of Jesus. It is He who lights every lamp, *i.e.*, who enlightens every individual Christian; and so it is His prerogative to place the lamp where it will give most light, *i.e.*, to appoint to the individual Christian a post and sphere of usefulness. If any one tries to contravene this appointment, preferring to keep such light as he has for his own comfort within his breast, he resists the revealed will of God. If he persists in this selfishness, his penalty is sure. The light that is in him will wax dim and incur great risk of going out, because it is shut up, and not set to burn on the lamp-stand, where the fresh air may reach and feed the flame.

In the early Christian centuries there was strong temptation to hide the light: and for such an ordeal Christ fortified His disciples in the words, "Blessed are ye when men shall reproach you and persecute you." But it must have required no small faith and fortitude to confess the name of Christ in the face of the world's hatred and contempt. It demanded the same type of holy courage as nerved the soul of Daniel when he knew that the decree was signed dooming every man of prayer to the lions' den, and yet at his open window "kneeled upon his knees three times a day, and prayed, and gave thanks before his God, as he did aforetime;" or as enabled "Peter and John," when arraigned before the Council which had condemned their Master, to proclaim His name before those "rulers of the people and elders of Israel." But God gave such courage to thousands of martyrs, so that the light was never extinguished even in the days of heaviest persecution. And He will give it in the future as He has given it in the past; for we have not yet arrived at the end of pitiless persecution for the name of Christ.

Even in communities that ring with boasts of freedom and praises of charity, earnest Christianity is still maltreated and reviled. Men are laughed at and stigmatised as pretentious hypocrites if they raise ever so modest a testimony to the Lord Jesus Christ. This is nothing to the ordeal through which many of the martyrs passed; and yet it is no slight trial to endure ridicule and misjudgment from one's equals and neighbours, and that for doing what the Lord has commanded —letting the light shine.

Among cultivated people especially there is a singular dread of anything which may be called very pronounced in religion. Persons who are not averse to make all the show they can in social life are wonderfully sensitive about any disclosure of spiritual conviction or feeling, object to go beyond a carefully measured form of words in religion, and would rather be taken for hesitating than for unhesitating and earnest Christians. Now there

never was a religious teacher who inveighed
more strongly than Jesus Christ did against
the temper of ostentation and the plague
of unreal professions of godliness; but while
He denounced the pretentious Scribes and
Pharisees, and Himself wore no phylactery,
was content to have the blue edge of His
dress of the ordinary width, and preferred
praying apart on a mountain to praying in
all men's sight at the corners of the streets,
He was the most open and fearless witness
for God in all the land. So should His followers be, whatever their worldly rank or
station; no Pharisees, no seekers of religious
notoriety for themselves, but frank, natural,
courageous, avowed witnesses to and servants
of the Lord Jesus.

The figure of the house-lamp suggests domestic Christianity; that of the conspicuous
city the more public and collective duty of
Christians.

Domestic Christianity! Home religion!
Is there anything more needed? It is a
mere mockery of this to have a house full
of vanity and discord, but with a daily

routine of family prayer.   In two of his
most profound and eloquent epistles, St.
Paul, proceeding from doctrine to practice,
exhorts to family religion ; and his directions are these : " Husbands, love your wives,
and be not bitter against them." " Wives,
submit yourselves to your own husbands, as
it is fit in the Lord."   " Parents, bring up
your children in the nurture and admonition
of the Lord." " Children, obey your parents
in the Lord, for this is right."   " Masters,
give to your servants that which is just and
equal." " Servants, obey in all things your
masters according to the flesh."   In such
unostentatious performance of mutual duties
does the house-lamp for Christ most brightly
shine ; and in such a household of love and
justice there is sweet concord.   Darkness
and tempest go together ; so do light and
peace.

The city on a hill, where it catches the
strong sunshine, is seen far and wide over
the plains ; and this suggests the collective
testimony of Christians. The Church which
they form has this for its lofty ideal,—

a city which has the glory of God and shines afar. Would that every particular Church were found thus telling on the surrounding population, and lighting up a whole region with a heavenly sheen! It may be the invisible Church as respects the secret of its life, power, and endurance in God; but it should be visible in its influence on society and its benevolent activities—" a city that cannot be hid."

We have seen that God places every lamp which He lights on some stand that it may shine to good purpose. It is, therefore, a sin against God to let cowardice or fastidiousness cover, or even half conceal, what was meant for manifestation. Add to this the positive statement of our Saviour to the effect that through the shining of Christians in the world their Father in heaven is glorified. He would have all those who, receiving the adoption of sons, become His brethren, to live, as He did, with this chief end in view—to glorify the Father; not only to please Him, but to draw the admiring and adoring thoughts of men to that Heavenly Father who is light, and in whom there is no darkness at all. No glory to the lamp! All praise and honour to Him who has lightened our darkness, and deigns to use us to lighten the darkness of the world!

The "good works" which our Lord expects and requires of all the children of the light are not laborious efforts of self-righteous men to secure their own salvation, but the works of faith and labours of love which proceed from men whom grace has saved—the appropriate manifestations of a renewed heart in temper, word, and action. They indicate the whole course of conduct which becomes the sons of God, and by which they shed abroad the light of goodness and truth. They are not to do good in order to be seen and commended by their fellow-men, but they are to do good that may be seen, that cannot but be seen, in order that their Father in heaven may be glorified.

Wanted, much wanted, bright Christians! Wanted for the glory of God, for the conviction of the world and silencing of gainsayers, who allege that Christianity has grown dim

and feeble! Wanted more frequent and in-
disputable examples of life actuated by high
motives and lustrous with the heavenly light
of faith and love!

III.

TREASURE.

"Lay not up for yourselves treasures upon the earth, where moth and rust doth consume, and where thieves break through and steal : but lay up for yourselves treasures in heaven, where neither moth nor rust doth consume, and where thieves do not break through nor steal : for where thy treasure is, there will thy heart be also."—St. Matt. vi. 19-21.

"Sell that ye have, and give alms ; make for yourselves purses which wax not old, a treasure in the heavens that faileth not, where no thief draweth near, neither moth destroyeth. For where your treasure is, there will your heart be also."—St. Luke xii. 33, 34.

Treasures on earth and treasures in heaven. The Lord's reference to the former is not metaphorical; they are actual, visible, and tangible objects of desire. No doubt, under the general term treasures, may be embraced earthly fame, rank, influence, and popularity, on all of which men are prone to set too high a value; but the language of Christ points directly to riches, which an Oriental was apt to invest in stores of costly raiment, or to hoard in the form of gold and jewels and precious vessels hidden in his house or under ground.

"Treasure not such treasures," He said to His disciples. "Sell that ye have and give alms." This was new doctrine, for the Pharisees, the most prominently religious men in the country, were covetous, and seemed to find no difficulty in serving both God and mammon.

Here is no condemnation of money or censure of those who grow rich. Christ lays on His followers no vow of poverty, nor may His great name be cited in support of communistic plans for compelling a distribution of wealth. What He has condemned is the treasuring of earthly possessions as if they were the only true riches and the highest good. They are not so, because they are earthly, and meet only temporal wants. They cannot be so, because they are uncertain and perishable. A little moth might eat away the costly silks and embroideries of the opulent Jew. A thief might break through the clay wall of the house, or dig down to the hiding-place, and make away with all the vessels of curious workmanship and the bags full of precious stones and metals.

Modern Western modes of keeping and investing money are different, but losses and disappointments are not prevented. Reverses of fortune are as common now as in any past age of the world. Nothing is easier than to let the desire of high interest and rapid accumulation tempt one into an investment which cannot be called a security except in irony; or, after acquiring a sum of money by patient industry, to put it in unsafe hands and lose it all at once through the fraud or default of others. Alas for those who "trust in uncertain riches!" In this life how are their hearts choked with cares of this world! And at death, how poor they are! They carry nothing with them.

We mark our contempt for a man who is infatuated about the possession of money by calling him miser; *i.e.,* wretch. Pope says—

"Pale Mammon pines amidst his store." *

Spenser represents him as an "uncouth wight," "sitting in secret shade"—

* Moral Essays, iii.

"And in his lap a mass of coin he told
And turned upside down, to feed his eye
And covetous desire with his huge treasury."*

In one of the best of his essays Montaigne tells how a passion for hoarding money possessed him at one period of his life, and plunged him in continual solicitude. "After you have once set your heart upon your heap it is no more at your service; you cannot find in your heart to break it; 'tis a building that you fancy must of necessity all tumble down to ruin if you stir but the least pebble."† As to the blindness of the money-lover to spiritual concerns, how graphic is the picture of a miser in the second part of the "Pilgrim's Progress!" The Interpreter showed to Christiana and her company a man who "could look no way but downwards," with a muck-rake in his hand. "There stood also one over his head with a celestial crown in his hand, and proffered him that crown for his muck-rake; but this man did neither look up nor regard, but raked to himself the straws, small sticks, and dust of the floor." The In-

* Faerie Queene, cant. vii. † Essays, chap. xl.

terpreter explained—"Earthly things, when they are with power upon men's minds, quite carry their hearts away from God. Then said Christiana, 'Oh deliver me from this muck-rake!'" *

It is very difficult to cure a man on whom the passion for earthly treasure has taken hold. He will listen to ever so many demonstrations of the folly and evil of covetousness, culled from literature and from observation of the world, but he will not depart from it. In fact, nothing will accomplish the cure of covetousness but the expulsive power of a new affection. A man who is risen with Christ has such an affection, and seeks those things which are above.

According to our Lord's metaphor, His followers are to treasure up treasures in heaven. This cannot mean to wish for high seats in heaven, with great lustre and distinction for themselves, for such desires may indicate nothing more than a new form of selfishness. The treasure must be of a more spiritual character, and such as a lowly heart may crave.

* Pilgrim's Progress, part ii.

It must be riches towards God and in God. It must mean the satisfaction of longings of the human spirit which the world cannot meet. It must be treasure of a calm conscience and a holy mind, resting in the love of God and sustained by the fellowship of the Spirit.

The portion of the wise deserves to be called treasure because it is (1.) so precious, (2.) in such safe keeping, and (3.) capable of indefinite increase.

1. Precious is this treasure, as meeting not the fancy of a day or even the wants of the passing years, but the most profound require-ments of the human soul, and that, too, when Divine regenerating grace has made it capable of eternal life and joy.

2. Secure is this treasure, as laid up in heaven above the risk of loss. And there the inheritance is not only uncorrupted, but in-corruptible; not only bright, but unfading; not only settled, but inalienable.

3. Capable of indefinite increase is this treasure. St. Paul has spoken of infatuated men, " who, after their hardness and impeni-tence, treasure up for themselves wrath in the

day of wrath and revelation of the righteous judgment of God." That woeful treasure, that evil portion, is capable of increase. Opposite to these, however, the Apostle places men who "by patience in well-doing seek for glory, honour, and incorruption." These are the heirs of eternal life.* And according to the measure of patience and well-doing is the accumulation of treasure in heaven.

Are we then, after all, to earn our own salvation? What has become of the doctrine of free grace? The answer is, that when our Lord spoke of laying up treasure, He was not treating of the justification of the ungodly, or the entrance on a state of salvation which is entirely of grace and not of works, lest any man should boast. He spoke of the amount of blessedness and degree of glory which men who are saved by grace are to obtain in heaven, and such amount or degree will be the reward of faithful service, the treasure accumulated by patient well-doing. It is a gracious reward, but it is a reward, and proportioned to the earthly obedience. So among men, who

* Romans ii. 5-7.

are alike saved by grace, there will be inequalities hereafter, as there are here and now. One has a smaller, another a greater treasure in heaven.

Alas! how little is heaven in the thoughts of men! how little in their hearts! Yet almost every one seems to think that, if there be a future state, he will somehow go to heaven. Heaven without a heavenward-tending mind! The prize of the high calling without running for it, or denying one's self in anything to obtain it! A vain confidence! When a man's heart is keen for earthly success or covered with the dust of worldly care, what treasure can he have in heaven? Where the treasure is, the heart is also; and where the heart is, there the treasure, if there be any, will be found.

In the year 1699, Dr. South preached on this theme before the University of Oxford. The sermon appears in his works under the title, "No man ever went to heaven whose heart was not there before," and is worth reading. It ends with a lamentation over

" the extreme vanity of most men's professions
of religion."   " We may with great boldness
affirm that if men would be at half the pains
to provide themselves treasures in heaven
which they are generally at to get estates
here on earth, it were impossible for any to
be damned.   But, when we come to earthly
matters, we do; when to heavenly, we only
discourse.   Heaven has our tongue's talk, but
the earth our whole man besides."

It may be a safe and prudent prayer in
regard to temporal things, "Give me neither
poverty nor riches," * but in things spiritual
we may pray, " Give me both poverty and
riches."   Let me have poverty of spirit, and,
at the call of God, buy the wine and milk
of the gospel " without money and without
price."   So let me be rich in the love of Christ
which passes knowledge.   " The Lord is my
portion, saith my soul;" and heaven is my
treasure-house.   The disappointments of this
present time and place have their compensa-
tion there.   Works of faith and deeds of mercy

* Proverbs xxx. 8.

have their recompense there. Self-denial has its hundred-fold reward; and afflictions for the cause of Christ and of righteousness meet not consolation only, but "an eternal weight of glory."

IV.

THE CHIP AND THE BEAM.

" And why beholdest thou the mote that is in thy brother's eye, but considerest not the beam that is in thine own eye? Or how wilt thou say to thy brother, Let me cast out the mote out of thine eye ; and lo, the beam is in thine own eye? Thou hypocrite, cast out first the beam out of thine own eye ; and then shalt thou see clearly to cast out the mote out of thy brother's eye."—St. Matt. vii. 3-5.

" And why beholdest thou the mote that is in thy brother's eye, but considerest not the beam that is in thine own eye? Or how canst thou say to thy brother, Brother, let me cast out the mote that is in thine eye, when thou thyself beholdest not the beam that is in thine own eye? Thou hypocrite, cast out first the beam out of thine own eye, and then shalt thou see clearly to cast out the mote that is in thy brother's eye."—St. Luke vi. 41, 42.

THE Lord Jesus exposed the prevailing faults of the Scribes and Pharisees, and showed His disciples that they should be quite otherwise minded. They should not be covetous of earthly gain, but lay up treasure in heaven. They should not be ostentatious, but pray secretly and give alms modestly. They should not be censorious, but be just and charitable in their estimate of others.

On this last point the Heavenly Teacher was earnest and explicit. We sometimes hear harsh judgments justified on the ground that those who form and express them know human nature well, and the unvarnished realities of life. But here speaks One who had the most absolute knowledge of what is in man, and could judge unerringly of actions and their motives, and His counsel is to beware of magnifying the faults of our neighbours, or indulging in harsh and hasty censures. To impress this lesson He used an illustration so apt that it has become one of the household phrases of Christendom. Indeed, many use it who scarcely know whence it is derived.

No one disputes that men who love righteousness must take note of unrighteous conduct, and must regard it with pain and disapproval. No one disputes, every one holds, that good men ought to take cognisance of the evil which is in the world, in order to track it to its sources and endeavour to apply correctives and remedies. The question now raised is about the temper in which this ought to be done, the clearness of the moral vision and the integrity and kindness of the moral purpose.

Jesus insisted on clearness of moral perception when He described the eye as "the lamp of the body," and laid emphasis on its singleness. Covetousness and all unbelieving anxiety about things temporal were to be shunned, because such feelings confused the eye of the mind. The same thing is true of a censorious disposition. It usually implies, and always fosters, self-ignorance and self-conceit. And the Lord so illustrated this as to bring out the unreasonable and even ludicrous aspect of Pharisaic censures. Two men meet, the one of whom has his eye almost closed by a large fragment of wood, here called the beam, while the other has got a small chip of wood in his eye. The word "mote" is well enough as indicating a very small size, but suggests dust, whereas it belongs to the aptness of the illustration that the obstruction to vision is of the same material in both men, but in the one very large, in the other comparatively trifling. Yet he who is scarcely able to see anything accurately because of the wood in his eye, beholds or stares at the eye of his brother, and proposes to remove that little chip—an operation on a most sensitive organ of the body, which would require clear vision and a steady hand. The thing would be absurd; those who heard our Saviour put the case in this way must have been moved as we are when we hear some blatant assumption pierced by a delicate sarcasm.

The case has only to be stated in order to carry the inference that he who has the large obstruction in his eye should first get rid of it, so that he may be fit to operate on his brother's eye. In other words, a man should have his own errors and faults corrected, in order that he may be able first to see clearly, and then to correct firmly and wisely the errors and faults of others.

I. *It is a delicate operation to correct the faults of other men.*

It may be likened to the feat of taking a chip of wood, a hair, or an insect's wing out of an inflamed eye. A clumsy operator may easily make things worse. So may a clumsy or unkind censor offend his brother, and do no good, but rather harm. All the greater is the delicacy if one undertakes the task as a volunteer. One may accept reproof from a person whom he regards as having a right to advise and even to rebuke, such as a parent in a family or a pastor in a Christian flock; or he may take it well from a private friend with whom he is on confidential terms, and whose counsel he has often sought; and yet he may not be at all willing to have his faults indicated and handled by any one who thinks proper to assume the function, and to constitute himself a fault-finder and fault-mender to society. It is only under an imperative sense of duty, and even then with the greatest diffidence, that a wise and humble man will venture this operation on one who, though a brother in the faith, is personally a stranger to him; for, even in the most favourable instance, the moral function which is attempted is a difficult one, and calls not only for a fine tact, but also for much self-knowledge in the operator, and much charity.

Something might be said here of the risk

that attends all human judgment of the conduct of other men. It is not often that one knows accurately and completely the outward facts, and one never quite knows the temptation resisted or yielded to, and the inward motive, or the commanding and determining one among a group of motives, which influenced the action under review. Considerations of this sort ought to be remembered as a corrective to severe judgment on the one hand, and to blind admiration on the other. But this is not the point before us. The case supposed is one of visible and undeniable fault. Still it is a delicate task to judge of it; it is a difficult operation to correct or remove it. It is of no use to gaze at it without trying to put it away; and he who would make such a trial needs to be himself good and wise. His eye must be clear, his conscience clean, his moral vision pure, who would see how to mend a brother's fault or take a mote out of a brother's eye.

II. *Self-ignorance and self-conceit incapacitate one for performing this operation.*

It cannot be said that faultiness in one's own character disables him as a critic of other men's morality. On the contrary, most accurate and pungent moral strictures may proceed from men who are quite aware that their own lives will not bear close inspection. There are men of broken character and bad habits who, writing anonymously for the press, show a keen perception of ethical distinctions, and lash the vices of the age with much vigour and effect. Nay more, men of the worst stamp are often found to have a wonderfully sharp eye for delinquencies on the part of their Christian neighbours, and are loud in condemnation of their shameful inconsistency. Such persons, it is true, care little for the correction of faults, but they see them clearly enough in the conduct of others, and exult in the thought that good people are not so good as they seem.

The case indicated by our Lord is that of one who is insensible of his own faultiness, yet presumes to deal with the faultiness of others ; and He addresses such a person by the strong term of disapproval, "hypocrite," which He often applied to the Scribes and Pharisees. Literally, it would be impossible for one who had even a small chip of wood in his eye to be unaware of it. The delicacy . of the organ would produce acute annoyance. But, alas! one may so destroy the delicacy of conscience as to go about with a great fault obvious to every one, and yet forget it, and suppose that no one else can see it. "Thou considerest not the beam that is in thine own eye." Such is the self-ignorance, begotten of pride, or rather of self-conceit, refusing to acknowledge what is disagreeable or discreditable—a foolish complacency which deceives no one.

If one thus blind to his own faults assumes to be a censor and corrector of morals, he plays the hypocrite in this sense, that he affects to be zealous for righteousness and impatient of evil, while all the while he excuses evil in himself, and condemns it only in others. It is a false zeal which flies at extraneous evil and spares that which is in our own homes, our own hearts and lives. First examine and arraign and amend thyself! First cast out the beam from thine own eye!

In the Canonical Book of Buddha there is a passage which exposes the same self-excusing habit that our Lord condemns. "The faults of others are easily perceived, but one's own faults it is difficult to perceive. A man winnows his neighbour's faults like chaff, but his own faults he hides, as a cheat hides the bad dice from the gambler." *

III. *An honest Christian reserves his strictest judgment for himself.*

Self-love will suggest excuses, and even tempt a man to ignore his own faults, or, at all events, to change their names; but a supreme love of righteousness, such as ought to possess the Christian mind, keeps conscience at work, and enjoins self-judgment and self-correction.

Then, as to the comparative seriousness of faults, there is a strong tendency to regard one's own misconduct with leniency, though

---

* Quoted in Bishop Titcomb's "Short Chapters on Buddhism," p. 166.

meting out a hard censure to similar delin-
quency in others. Ours is the mote or chip,
and our neighbour's is the beam. But when
the spirit of Christ enters into us, all this is
changed. Ours is the beam; our iniquity is
great; our fault is heinous. We know what
checks and warnings we have had to keep us
from it, what remonstrances of conscience, and
what impulses and examples to counteract the
evil temptation. And yet we are at fault.
Nay, we have persisted in what we know to
be wrong till it has acquired the force of a
habit, neutralising good, and unfitting us to
exert a healthy moral and religious influence
on others. The beam is in our own eye. It
is our neighbour who has the mote or chip.

So at least it should appear to us in the
judgment of charity. By this is not at all
meant that we are to make light of evil, or
out of good nature affect not to see what is
censurable. It is not charity, but a morbid
feebleness of the moral nature, which cannot
bear to condemn anything but strictness, and
glibly excuses or lightly tolerates conduct that
is vicious or dishonest. Nothing in our Lord's

teaching may or can be construed into a sanction of that species of leniency which makes all its allowance on the dangerous side. On the contrary, it is required by our loyalty to Him and to the best interests of society that we endeavour to maintain in ourselves and promote in others a moral tone that is brisk and vigorous, honouring the virtues of truth, justice, and purity, and reprobating the opposite vices. But there is no reason why this tone of rigorous discrimination between good and evil should not be combined with a gentle and charitable judgment of the character and motives of our neighbours and fellow-Christians. We are not competent to weigh their actions, for the reason already given, that our information is almost always partial, and also because our censure is very apt to be unduly aggravated if we happen to be ourselves in an uncomfortable mood, or if we have a feeling of personal dislike to those whose conduct is impugned. Nay, more, when a particular point of behaviour or line of conduct is under censure, and is confessedly indefensible, it is not easy for us to fix the degree of condemnation which it deserves, because we cannot say how much is due to wickedness, and how much to weakness, silliness, or misguidance. Sometimes behaviour that wears a most objectionable aspect proceeds from an ungracious manner, or a giddy mood, or bad taste, rather than bad intention. To a severe temper that may appear a huge beam which a kinder heart and more considerate judgment will be content to regard as a mote or small chip, which love and patience may remove.

"Have fervent charity among yourselves, for charity covereth a multitude of sins." * Such was the rule for the early Christians, and it is as much in force as ever. There is no religion that goes so deep as ours into the exposure of human sin and consequent misery, or has a moral tone so firm and vigorous ; but at the same time there is none that is so pervaded with the spirit of kindness and hopefulness. It charges us to forbear and forgive, and above all things, to "put on love, which is the bond of perfectness." †

* 1 Peter iv. 8.   † Coloss. iii. 13, 14.

V.

THE DOGS AND THE SWINE.

"Give not that which is holy unto the dogs, neither cast your pearls before the swine, lest haply they trample them under their feet, and turn and rend you."—ST. MATT. vii. 6.

IT is not an easy thing to be morally and spiritually useful to other men. It requires much more than holy talk. In our last chapter we have seen that it needs self-knowledge and charity — a recognition and removal of 'our own faults in order to discern and correct the faults of others. Now follows another lesson, to the effect that Christian usefulness requires careful discrimination of what is fitting or unfitting, and a power of reserve as well as a faculty of speech.

Perhaps it strikes some readers of the New Testament that the language used by our Lord in the text at the head of this chapter is scarcely worthy of such a teacher. They may urge that it was neither kind nor dignified to call men, however ungodly, dogs and swine. Is it not a duty to honour all men? But here lies a mistake. Our Saviour did not call men by opprobrious names. It is one thing, and not a very respectful thing, to call a man a sheep; quite another thing to illustrate the wandering of a sinful man from God by the straying of a sheep from the shepherd's care. So it would indeed be a harsh mode of speaking to stigmatise men as dogs and swine, as vile and stupid animals; but it is quite another thing to introduce such creatures in order to give point to an illustration of what would be unbecoming and unsuitable in the delivery of sacred truth to profane persons. It would be as incongruous and improper as to cast the sacrificial flesh from the altar to a street dog, or to throw pearls before a savage boar.

The first case supposed is that of a priest or Levite, who on leaving the temple observed one of the ever-hungry dogs that prowled about the city of Jerusalem, but were never admitted within the gates of the sanctuary. Forgetting all considerations of manners and propriety, he returned into the court, took a portion of flesh which had been on the altar of burnt-offering, and threw it to the dog. Such an action would violate the Divine law which assigned the flesh of the offerings to the priests, and it would indicate gross disrespect and a want of the sense of fitness. The fault found is not with the dog, which could know no better than snap up the piece of flesh. It was with the thoughtless or presumptuous priest.

The other case supposed is that of a lavish rich man, who, for some whim, or intending a practical joke, threw pearls, as if they were seeds, before a herd of swine. The swine in Palestine never were tame creatures, as with us. Though in some parts of the country they were kept in herds, they were by the Jewish law unclean animals, and disallowed as food for man. Accordingly they were at the most only half-tamed; and the genuine wild boar has always haunted the valley of the Jordan. Now, if one should cast pearls in the way supposed before those animals, they might rush for what seemed to be grain, since they are always voracious, but, quickly discovering the hoax, would trample on the pearls, as pigs commonly put their feet into and upon their food; and, not improbably, an enraged boar would rend the foolish man who had played this dangerous game by a side upward stroke of his tusk, as the manner of such creatures is. This turning and rending Horace refers to in one of his odes, where he alludes to the boar " obliquum meditantis ictum "—meditating a side-long thrust.*

What need, it may be asked, to warn respectable people against conduct like this, so profane, or so senseless and foolhardy? The answer is that extreme instances are chosen in order to put a much-needed lesson in a strong light, just as the warning against the self-complacency of a censorious man is given by supposing the case of one who had a large splinter of wood in his eye yet thought that he could see well enough to perform a delicate operation on the eye of his brother;

* Carm. iii. 22.

or as the case of a cruel father, who gives his child a serpent for a fish, is used to enhance by contrast the fatherly goodness of God.

But what is the lesson? It cannot be that Christians are never to press the Gospel on an indifferent, unsympathetic, or even hostile audience. In that case it would contradict all those counsels and charges which require a fearless and even an aggressive testimony to the name of Jesus; and it would be at variance with the example of our Lord and His apostles, who preached the Word in the face of angry opposition. Christ did not reserve Himself for well-disposed hearers, nor did His disciples. Did not St. Peter, with his friend St. John by his side, preach Jesus as the Christ to the Council at Jerusalem which had condemned Jesus within a few weeks, and had arrested the two apostles for the offence of speaking to the people in that name? Did not St. Paul, with similar intrepidity, preach to the mocking Athenians, and to the angry crowd at Jerusalem, from whose clutches he had just been rescued by the Roman soldiers? And since those days, how many brave witnesses for

Christ have proclaimed repentance and salvation to men who hated them and hooted at their testimony! It cannot be that those are condemned by any saying of their Lord. He never can have intended to pluck heroism and martyrdom out of Christian service. On the contrary, the courageous and heroic temper is in full harmony with the spirit of Jesus Christ and His gospel. There can scarcely be too much boldness in making known the love and the will of God. If opponents have not merely neglected the gospel, but met it with the violence of persecution; if they have turned and rent as with a wild boar's tusk those who sought to do them good, the Lord does not censure, but will certainly reward those who suffered for His name, perhaps lost their lives for His sake, and that of His gospel.

The positive lesson conveyed in this metaphorical saying of Jesus is one of reverence and discretion. We understand it thus :—

I. *As to the preaching of the gospel.*

While the preacher is not to evade difficulty or shrink from opposition or personal danger, he is to consult decorum and opportunity so far as not to expose names and things that are sacred to open and egregious contempt. On this principle one is not to address religious truth to a drunkard in his cups, or to him who sits in the scorner's chair. It is true that cases have been known in which the truth wonderfully sobered the drunkard or silenced the scoffer; but no such rare instances justify an unseemly subjection of the name and Word of God to an overwhelming risk of jibe and blasphemy. Open-air preaching, too, requires very especially to be placed under this rule of Christ. If conducted at fit places and times, it is not merely an allowable, but a highly commendable practice; but the question of fitness is of far more importance than inexperienced preachers are aware. To our thinking, it does not well consist with the precept of Christ now under our consideration for one to enter into a sort of shouting competition with hucksters at the corner of a busy street, or to pray and preach in the throng and hubbub of a race-course. Can it be reconciled with any proper feeling of reverence that ears which are filled with the cry of some seller of cheap wares by the side-walk, or the voice of a singer of ribald ballads, or with the roar of men offering bets, or the coarse jokes and hideous swearing of "roughs," should in the midst of all this hear a rival vociferation of such names as Jesus and the Holy Ghost, with ever so many well-meant appeals for repentance and faith? We do not deny that in an occasional, very occasional, instance, good has been done by such venturesome preaching; but no one can tell on the other side how much harm has been done by breaking down the sense of reverence, and exposing what is more holy and precious than the best men are able to conceive to the open scorn, or, what may be even worse, the unchastened familiarity, of the foolish and the profane.

II. *As to statements of spiritual experience.* In this matter Christian men are apt to fall into one or other of two opposite extremes. Many pass through life with hardly a word, even to their pastors or their nearest friends, which indicates that they have received any spiritual benefit or have any inward experience of the grace of God. This is the one extreme of unreasonable reticence. On the other hand, a good many talk too much about themselves, and will even volunteer before indiscriminate assemblies an account of their conversion, and of their great peace and joy in believing. This is the opposite, the egotistical extreme ; and none the less egotistical that the statement is accompanied with many exclamations of " Glory to God ! "

Between these extremes the wise and humble Christian ought to steer his course. He must consider his company and his opportunity. If he be among those who fear God and have some personal acquaintance with the spiritual life, he may " tell what God has done for his soul," so as to strengthen his brethren and stir them up to love and praise. If he be in a mixed company, he will probably be more reserved. If he be among persons unfit to estimate holy and precious things, he will not cast religious experience before them, to be misconstrued and possibly trampled under foot. The work of the Holy Spirit in us is to be submitted only to spiritual men, and even to them should always be disclosed with lowliness and modesty.

III. *As to the admission to sacred privileges and functions in the Church.*

It is a degradation and misuse of holy ordinances to press them on persons of unjust or impure lives. True that in our modern Christendom it is not possible for Church-rulers to draw an absolute line of separation between the holy and the profane. There must be broad margins of forbearance, and charity hopes all things; but it would be a disastrous error to surrender the great principle of Church separation and discipline, that holy things are for the holy. Such is the principle on which St. Paul proceeded when he charged the Corinthian Christians not to retain in fellowship "a fornicator, or covetous, or an idolater, or a reviler, or a drunkard, or an extortioner." * "Be ye not unequally yoked with unbelievers." †

* 1 Cor. v. 11.   † 2 Cor. vi. 14.

The Reformed Churches in the sixteenth century were honourably distinguished by their revival of Church discipline. They required, with the reformation of faith and worship, also a reform of manners and morals. In the Book of Common Order of the Church of Scotland (A.D. 1560) occurs this weighty paragraph :—

"There are three causes, chiefly, which move the Church of God to the executing of discipline : — (1.) That men of evil conversation be not numbered among God's children, to their Father's reproach, as if the Church of God were a sanctuary for naughty and vile persons. (2.) That the good be not infected by the evil, which thing St. Paul foresaw when he commanded the Corinthians to banish from among them the incestuous adulterer, saying, 'A little leaven maketh sour the whole lump of dough.' (3.) That a man thus corrected or excommunicated might be ashamed of his fault, and so through repentance come to amendment."

The confusion into which Christian society has fallen makes it difficult for the most faithful Churches to apply the sound principle of the separation of the holy from the unclean. Churches that have lost or surrendered the power of self-discipline enfeeble discipline in other Churches also. But none the less does it remain a sacred duty to warn from the Lord's table the carnally-minded and such as do not discern the Lord's body, and never knowingly to admit to Church privilege or office any who are of impure or intemperate habits. Such persons there were in the first ages, naming the name of the Lord, and then turning back "from the holy commandment." St. Peter refers to such in terms which recall an ancient proverb,* but also have an unquestionable reminiscence of the saying of Jesus about the dogs and swine, which the Apostle, having once heard, could never forget—"The dog turning to his own vomit again, and the sow that had washed to wallowing in the mire." †

The Lord make clean our hearts within us, and then " give us His own flesh to eat!" It is meat indeed, for it is the flesh of the Sacri-

* Prov. xxvi. 11.　　　　† 2 Peter ii. 22.

fice once offered for us. Then will the pearls of sacred truth be recognised by us as precious. We know of one pearl of great price, and gladly sell all that we have in order to possess that pearl.

VI.

TWO GATES AND TWO WAYS.

"Enter ye in by the narrow gate: for wide is the gate, and broad is the way, that leadeth to destruction, and many be they that enter in thereby. For narrow is the gate, and straitened the way, that leadeth unto life, and few be they that find it."—St. Matt. vii. 13, 14.

In all times and all languages human life has been likened to a journey. The Bible has many examples. Enoch walked with God. Jacob described the years of his life as the years of his pilgrimage. St. Paul referred to men who "walked according to the course of the world," denounced "walking after the flesh," and commended "walking in the Spirit." It is a common usage to speak of a way of life or a course of conduct; and so there is no difficulty in understanding that when Jesus Christ employed in His teaching the illustration of two gates and two roads, He meant to indicate two modes and tendencies of human life. In fact, He put vividly before His audience the same alternative which a great painter put on the canvas in the rival persuasions of Minerva and Venus —Wisdom and Pleasure—appealing from opposite sides to inexperienced and impulsive youth.

It is a bold and comprehensive generalisation. As they appear to us, the paths of human conduct are very various. We cannot reduce them to two, or pronounce confidently that this man is on the sure road to heaven, and that man on the sure way to hell; but under all the moral shades and circumstantial diversities of human life our Lord saw two opposite lines of tendency, and only two. The one is the way of the unjust, the other the path of the just. The one is the way of the flesh, and the other the path of the Spirit.

I. A wide gate lying open invites your entrance, and a broad smooth avenue gives promise of leading you to some mansion, castle, or pleasure-ground. Such is the gate and such is the way of self-indulgence—at the outset of life easy to the feet, pleasant to the eye, seductive to the senses and the imagination.

The pleasure, indeed, is only for a season. The way becomes rough, and for one who continues on it smiling to the last, you may find seven grumbling and out of humour. The road of pleasure is infested with stinging nettles of pain. Wounded pride, satiated appetite, foiled ambitions, disappointed plans, gnawing jealousies, spoil everything this world can furnish. "Vanity of vanities : all is vanity." Still men go on in the broad way. Their choice has been made, their habits are formed ; they must just get as much as they can out of their lives on the line which they have adopted. If they feel, as sometimes they must, that they are by no means making the best thing possible out of their life and opportunities, they try to console themselves by the thought that they are not singular in this. They are as good as most of their neighbours, and live as people of their rank are wont to do. If life, as it proceeds, disappoints their hopes, they suffer only the common lot.

It is one of the inducements to men to

enter the wide gate, that "many go in thereat." Men are very gregarious, and the crowd always draws a greater crowd. It is comparatively rare to find a man act strictly from individual convictions and think out his line of conduct from his own reason and conscience. Most men copy one another. So, because the broad way has been the popular way, it becomes more and more popular. A new generation throng the gate, following the steps of their fathers, as their fathers followed their predecessors, each generation finding, as they finish the course, and it is too late to alter it, to what a woeful termination the broad way has conducted them.

"Leadeth to destruction." So said the Faithful and True Witness. He did not set Himself to prove the statement, or enter into any argument to show that such is the necessary conclusion to a life of self-seeking and self-indulgence. He was not a reasoner, but a revealer. He saw the end from the beginning, and declared it with the calm authority of one who had complete cognisance of the issues of life in good and evil, in weal and woe. He knew, and therefore gave warning, that the "broad way" leads to no sweet home or celestial palace, but to a beetling precipice and sore destruction.

From this there is a possibility of escape; but at the beginning, not at the end. One must turn away from the inviting gate and dare to dissent from the multitude; or, if he has unhappily entered the gate and proceeded on the way, he must, at the warning of Christ, be converted; he must turn, retrace his steps in repentance, and come out through the gate, reversing the very principle of his life, that he may enter on a new course before it is too late.

II. A narrow gate is overlooked by the crowd, or is avoided because it opens on a mere footpath closely hedged or walled in on either side. The presumption is that it leads to a poor man's cottage or a cattle-shed. True that over the gate indicated by Christ those who believe His Word may see an inscription, "To the Palace of the King." But the heedless multitude do not see this inscription, or, if their attention is called to it, make light of it, persuading themselves that there must be much easier and more conspicuous avenues to the palace.

There is a passage in the Second Book of Esdras which resembles the saying of Jesus Christ now under our consideration, but the date of that book being quite uncertain, we cannot even put it as a conjecture that our Lord may have had the words of Esdras in His mind. The inheritance of God's people is likened to " a city set upon a broad field, and full of all good things, but the entrance is narrow and set in a dangerous place, as if there were a fire on the right hand, and on the left a deep water, and only one path between these, so small that but one man at once could go there." Then follows the question, " If this city were given unto a man for an inheritance, if he never shall pass through the danger set before it, how shall he receive this inheritance ? " *

It is not danger that our Lord's language suggests so much as the need of humility, self-denial, and non-conformity to the world.

* 2 Esdras vii.

One must repent and humble himself as a little child in order to pass through the gate and enter on the way. Thereafter, too, he must maintain a high purpose and a firm self-control in order to advance on the way, on no account deviating from the path of righteousness, however tempting the "bypath meadows" may be. After all, those soft meadows of ease and compromise are more mischievous than the ditches, into which if a man fall he is defiled, or the fire and water on either side, which compel vigilance.

Mark the entire frankness with which Jesus Christ proclaimed the difficulty of being one of His disciples and walking in the way of His steps. Evidently He was conscious of a right to command the allegiance of men at whatever cost, and of a power to recompense those who might suffer for His name and "for righteousness' sake." The way which He set before His followers might be arduous, but there were and would always be ample compensations for all the difficulties and temporal losses which it might entail. No lion or ravenous beast goes up on that way of holiness.* Angels encamp round about it, and the Holy Spirit, the Comforter, leads all those who walk thereon.

Add to this, that the narrow way is brightened by the promise and hope of eternal life which we have in Christ Jesus. It will not end, like the broad way, in a precipice hanging over the pit of death. Nor is the issue of it in a mere vague futurity, like that of the woodland path to which an American poet compares human life—

> "On a trackless beach,
> With a boundless sea before." †

The narrowed way broadens into a sure and glorious issue. It leads to life. Of ordinary human existence, we say that it leads to, it ends in, death; but the life of faith and new obedience passes into a fuller and higher vitality — the life everlasting. No mention here of deathbeds or graves, because these come to men, or men come to them, in a natural order apart altogether from Christ. Life in Him is not interrupted by the de-

* Isa. xxxv. 9.   † Bryant's Later Poems, *The Unknown Way.*

cease and dissolution of the body, nor is there any interception of its progress toward its heavenly expansion and fulness in the presence of the King.

Yet what mournful words are these that follow!—" Few there be that find it." There are two mistakes, opposite to each other, to be avoided :—

1. They misconstrue the Scriptures who infer from the expression just quoted that the saved of the Lord in every generation must be few. Christ stated a melancholy fact in regard to His own generation, who "received Him not," but did not predict that the same state of matters would last throughout all generations. After the same manner He addressed His followers as a "little flock;" but did not therein imply that His flock would always be small. William Cowper, however, had evidently been taught so·; and, accordingly, in one of his hymns, the Saviour of a multitude that no man can number is addressed as—

" Dear Shepherd of Thy chosen few."

A similar misuse is often made of St.
Paul's observation, that not many of the
mighty, the noble, or the wise in the heathen
world were among "the called," or in Christian fellowship,* and that the Church received her reinforcements more frequently
from those classes of society which had less
repute and influence.   He stated this as a
fact of the time, and one which the Corinthians to whom he wrote might see for themselves; but he did not lay it down as a
principle or standing law of Christianity for
all time coming.   Yet this inference seems
often to be drawn; and a false impression
is conveyed that our religion has an antipathy to culture, and that it is more adapted
to the ignorant than to men of education and
refinement.

In the instance before us, our Lord pointed
out that few in His time chose the way of
righteousness; but whether in the end only
a few would be saved, He said not.   When
the question was put to Him, He declined
to answer it, but told the questioners to look

* 1 Cor. i. 26.

well to themselves, lest they should miss the entrance. "Strive ye to enter in." *

2. They err on the other side who think it due to charity to suppose that all or nearly all men are to be saved. It is from Holy Scripture only that sound knowledge on such a point can be derived ; and Scripture throughout gives us to understand that not all mankind, but a people taken from out the mass of mankind, are and are to be saved. No teacher within all the bounds of Holy Writ is more clear to this effect than the Master Himself. We can make nothing of the solemn alternatives laid down by Him if it is to be held that those who love the world and follow the common course of self-pleasing, shutting God out of their thoughts, are nevertheless in a state of safety and in the path to life.

It is weak, and worse than weak, to refrain from warning men against incurring perdition, lest we be thought uncharitable. The matter is not one to be settled by our dispositions or wishes. The Judge of all the earth will

* St. Luke xiii. 23, 24.

do right. We have to hold and proclaim, not what we desire, but what He has told us. It is right to be charitable, but no one needs be more charitable than Jesus Christ. It is well to be liberal, but with one's own things, not those of another. It is a cheap and hollow liberality that is always ready to give way on the truths of God's Word, and to yield the claims of His righteousness.

Charity and liberality of mind teach us to put the kindest construction on the motives of our fellow-men, and to hope the best that is credible concerning them, but do not authorise us to contradict the Bible, or confuse moral and spiritual distinctions that involve inevitably opposite issues. Both the express words and the warning tone of Jesus and His apostles announce to us a real danger of perdition, and bid us and all strive to enter in at the gate, and abide in the way of salvation.

However plainly the alternative is put, some will "halt between two opinions." They demur to being put in such a dilemma, and urged to a firm and prompt decision. There seems to be a vague hope afloat that this clever and advanced generation may manage to combine the broad way and the narrow, or strike out a third path which will unite all advantages while obviating discomfort and singularity. It will be worldliness made safe and godliness made easy. But all this is folly. The two gates and two ways described with unerring wisdom by our Lord are incapable of combination or compromise. If a man love the world, the love of the Father is not in him. If a man lead the life of a sinner, he cannot die the death or gain the inheritance of a saint.

VII.

TREES AND THEIR FRUIT.

" Beware of false prophets, which come to you in sheep's clothing, but inwardly are ravening wolves. By their fruits ye shall know them. Do men gather grapes of thorns, or figs of thistles? Even so every good tree bringeth forth good fruit ; but the corrupt tree bringeth forth evil fruit. A good tree cannot bring forth evil fruit, neither can a corrupt tree bring forth good fruit. Every tree that bringeth not forth good fruit is hewn down, and cast into the fire. Therefore by their fruits ye shall know them."—St. Matt. vii. 15-20.

" For there is no good tree that bringeth forth corrupt fruit; nor again a corrupt tree that bringeth forth good fruit. For each tree is known by its own fruit. For of thorns men do not gather figs, nor of a bramble bush gather they grapes."—St. Luke vi. 43, 44.

The comparison of men to fruit-trees is a very obvious one, and of frequent occurrence in the Bible. Every tree brings forth after its kind. Every man acts according to his prevailing disposition and will. Thus from the fruit you can tell the nature of the tree which has produced it; and from his course of conduct you may tell the kind of man you have to deal with. He is a good tree, a tree planted by the rivers of water, a fruitful olive-tree, a flourishing palm-tree, a tree of righteousness; or he is a corrupt tree, a withered tree, a dry tree.

One of the chief dangers which beset primitive Christianity was the intrusion of false prophets. There were men who affected to bear a message from God, while He had not sent them; but in those days of inexperience and open testimony, they found the ear of Christian congregations, and "crept into houses, beguiling unstable souls." They were without the knowledge and experience of the truth, but made their way by plausible protestations and flattering words. The Epistles are full of allusions to such men, as misleading the Churches.

The delusive professions of the false prophets and teachers were only so much "sheep's clothing" worn for a purpose. Christ's servants in a hostile world were as sheep in the midst of wolves; but those deceivers were wolves in the midst of the sheep, serving themselves of the flock, not obedient to the Heavenly Shepherd. In this they showed what nature they were of. Clothe a wolf in sheep-skins, still he will ravin. Call a tree by what name you choose, it will bring forth fruit after its own kind. They are not grapes, but bitter black berries that grow on the buckthorn, and thistles yield no figs.

The early Churches were required to protect themselves from the false teachers. Apostles could not be everywhere to test every one who claimed to address the Christian assemblies. So the brethren were to exercise a wise and necessary caution, and not hearken to every teacher or believe every spirit. St. Paul wrote to the Galatians that they ought to have rejected any one, even though he were of an angelic attractiveness, who preached a gospel at variance with that which had been delivered to them. St. John exhorted Christians at the end of the first century to "prove the spirits whether they are of God," and especially to watch the doctrine concerning Jesus Christ as "come in the flesh."

The development of doctrine had not proceeded so far when our Lord taught on the Mount, and His reference to the fruit-trees indicates a practical and not a dogmatic test. See how it applies—

I. *To the teachers of religion.*

We do not admit that there were no doctrinal tests in the apostolic times. The references we have just made to the writings of two of the chief apostles prove the contrary. But the moral test was a primary one, and could be applied by any man with a correct sense of right and wrong, even though he might not be much versed in theology. And the apostles followed their Master in urging on the Churches the application of this moral test. St. Paul often referred to the selfish motives and immoral lives of those unauthorised and perverse teachers who tried to undermine his influence, at the same time reminding the Churches of his personal conduct and example among them. St. Peter denounced the licentiousness and covetousness of the same class of men. St. John, in his significant manner, wrote, "He that doeth evil hath not seen God." St. Jude pointed with severe reprobation to "ungodly men" who were troubling the Churches— "walking after their lusts, and their mouth speaketh great swelling words."

It is true that a bad man may speak good words, having learned them from books or from other men; but he is not, therefore, to be accepted as a religious teacher. Every one who does righteousness is begotten of God. He who does it not, is not of God, and has no claim to speak for God. However unexceptionable his doctrine, his influence cannot be safe or healthy. In fact, he brings dishonour to the doctrine and injury to the Church which listens to him. The corrupt tree brings forth evil fruit.

II. *To religious systems.*

Religion, however taught, must stand or fall according to the moral effect it produces on those who embrace and obey it. On this principle Christianity may boldly invite comparison with any form of heathenism, with Mohammedanism, or with the negation of religion.

in Materialism and Secularism. Imperfectly as it has been reduced to practice, it has led to a standard of private and public morals, an estimate of domestic virtue, an appreciation of righteousness, and a temper of mercy far beyond what can be shown under any other system. Indeed, the imperfection with which Christianity has been illustrated and obeyed by its own adherents may be cited as one of the proofs of its lofty origin. It is comparatively easy to be a thorough exponent and example of heathenism or Mohammedanism; but where can you find a perfect Christian? There is a consummate Christ: there are no consummate Christians. But in so far as men follow Christ and are imbued with His Spirit, they are good, virtuous, righteous. On the other hand, you cannot say that the more thoroughly heathen a man is, or the more intensely Mohammedan, or the more decidedly materialistic and secularistic in his convictions, the more sure he is to be good, virtuous, righteous. Judged by the fruit it produces where it flourishes, Christianity is the good tree.

The same test will lead to just conclusions regarding the rival forms of Christianity, provided always that a sufficiently large induction of instances be taken, and that time enough has been given for the working out of genuine results. It is not difficult to show that what may be called the sacerdotal form of Christianity bears this test badly. It has trained its votaries to devout practices and ecclesiastical submission; but its moral discipline, through the confessional and the imposition of penance, has wrought on the fear of penalty rather than on the healthy sense of right and wrong, while the casuistry applied to actions and the weighing and measuring of sins by the priests have tended to lower and confuse rather than to educate and strengthen conscience. The fruit is notorious in the unsatisfactory criminal statistics of a Roman Catholic as contrasted with a Protestant population. The tree is known by its fruit.

Let it be confessed that Protestant Christianity, even in its most earnest and evangelical form, leaves still much to be desired in the production of practical righteousness;

but at all events it is the right kind of tree. The gospel which is its glory is the doctrine according to godliness. The saving grace of God which it holds fast and holds forth is that which leads men to " live soberly, righteously, and godly in this present world."

A high moral influence is sometimes claimed for what may be called Unitarian and Rationalistic Christianity; and it should be freely acknowledged that this has been the religion of some most amiable, benevolent, and virtuous men. But the fruit or sure result of a system of belief and worship is to be estimated on a long issue and a large scale; and the history of the system now indicated shows its tendency to weaken the grasp of revealed religion on the human soul, and to leave with men nothing but a code of virtue and the praise of charity. Therefore it is powerless to rescue the perishing, to elevate the masses, to comfort the poor, or to restrain the rich from a refined but selfish luxury.

III. *To all men.*

In this sense the saying is often applied,

and has become a sort of moral adage—
"The tree is known by its fruit."

Application of such a text to our fellow-men must of course be with caution and charity. Great injury is done every day through a rash habit of judging on deficient or erroneous information, or through misconception springing from personal or party antipathies. First let us be sure of our facts; then, if it is our duty to judge at all, let us proceed on those facts as the evidences of character. Let us look not at leaves, but at fruit. And let us not be too severe on youthful faults. Trees sometimes yield poor and even bitter fruit when they are young which give sweet and finely flavoured fruit when they come to maturity.

Some estimate of our fellow-men we must form in order to guide our own behaviour towards them, and to warrant our trust or distrust. Then let our estimate depend not on professions, words, or appearances, all of which may be deceptive, but on solid actions and the sustained tenor of life. Let us mark what a man does or refuses to do, how he stands with those who must know him best, and what is the kind of influence he habitually exerts. We cannot go wrong in judging the tree by its fruit.

The same test may be used in self-judgment. No doubt a man may take himself to account in a way which he cannot apply to his neighbour. He may sift his own secret motives and scrutinise his most hidden thoughts and desires. He ought to know himself better than he can know any one else. Yet an honest man, trying to prove and judge himself, may be perplexed. It is hard to know the predominant motive or to detect the relative strength of desires that have twined together in the mind. Then comes in well this practical test, What, on the whole, is the bent of the character and will? What are the ends for which one lives day after day? Is right doing regarded as the imperative thing, or is the obligation practically modified by considerations of ease, of pleasure, or of immediate profit? A wise man will bring the question to the proof, recognising that only good fruit can authenticate a good fruit-tree.   A good man, in so far as he can stand this great test, will humbly and heartily disown all merit, and ascribe all that is morally and spiritually right in him to the renewing and sanctifying power of the Holy Ghost.

Nothing but a good tree can produce good fruit. It is impossible to manufacture it. Sometimes the doctrine of regeneration is represented as fanatical and impossible; but it is sound philosophy to begin at the root.   Interior disposition must determine exterior conduct and action. It is the glory and triumph of our religion that it provides for this. God is able to "make the tree good;" and then the good tree is known by its spontaneous fruit.

VIII.

THE WISE BUILDER AND THE FOOLISH.

"Every one therefore which heareth these words of mine, and doeth them, shall be likened unto a wise man, which built his house upon the rock : and the rain descended, and the floods came, and the winds blew, and beat upon that house ; and it fell not: for it was founded upon the rock. And every one that heareth these words of mine, and doeth them not, shall be likened unto a foolish man, which built his house upon the sand : and the rain descended, and the floods came, and the winds blew, and smote upon that house ; and it fell : and great was the fall thereof. And it came to pass, when Jesus ended these words, the multitudes were astonished at His teaching : for He taught them as one having authority, and not as their scribes."—ST. MATT. vii. 24-29.

"Every one that cometh unto me, and heareth my words, and doeth them, I will show you to whom he is like : he is like a man building a house, who digged and went deep, and laid a foundation upon the rock : and when a flood arose, the stream brake against that house, and could not shake it: because it had been well builded. But he that heareth, and doeth not, is like a man that built a house upon the earth without a foundation ; against which the stream brake, and straightway it fell in ; and the ruin of that house was great."—ST. LUKE vi. 47-49.

MOSES descended a terrible mountain in the wilderness, bringing the law for Israel inscribed on tablets of stone. The Prophet "like unto Moses" sat on a mountain of Palestine in the sunshine, with His disciples and the multitude listening while He opened His mouth in blessings, and then proceeded to indicate the deeper meanings of the Divine law, and to explain the righteousness which belongs to the Divine kingdom among men.

Sore punishments were denounced against those "who despised Moses's law." A grave responsibility fell on those who heard Christ's teaching on the Mount. So in closing His discourse, He warned His hearers not to think it enough to pay an outward respect to His instruction. They should be doers of the Word, and not hearers only.

The admonition is for all who read His words, as much as for those who originally heard them. It is much needed; for scarcely any part of Scripture has been more praised and less obeyed than the Sermon on the Mount. "Was it," one has well asked, "with the depressing foresight how much patronising admiration and barren praise would be expended on this sermon by men who shall never see the kingdom of God, that He was moved to close with darkening face in words like these, ' Every one that heareth these words of mine, and doeth them not, shall be likened to a foolish man, who built his house upon the sand' ? "

The peroration of the sermon employs a double illustration, which must have told with graphic power on an audience accustomed to the sudden tempests and sweeping floods of the climate of Judea.

I. *The two builders.*

A wise man, or one who acts prudently, is described as building a house. He looks well to the foundation, chooses one that will not sink and cannot be washed away. In such a country as Palestine it was the best policy to build upon a bed of solid rock.

In contrast to the wise builder is the foolish man, who gives no heed to the choice of a foundation, but goes to work on a loose and treacherous sand. He may erect an imposing mansion ; but what is the value of show without safety ?

1. To the former of these "shall be likened"

the obedient hearer of the words of Christ. To some this mode of describing a Christian appears to be scarcely evangelical. It seems to lay stress on doing, and not on believing. But in reality to " do the words" and to believe on Him who uttered them are not different actions of the mind, but essentially one and the same. It should be observed that the Sermon on the Mount was delivered at an early stage of our Lord's career, when He showed Himself in Galilee as a prophet. In that capacity He spoke, and the proper mode in which to express faith in Him was to hearken to His sayings and keep them. When He came to be more fully revealed in His saving purpose and power, more emphasis was laid on faith in Him. Those who follow Him are disciples, as He is their Teacher; believers, as He is their Saviour.

In fact, it is the adherence of the whole heart and mind to the Lord Jesus that is essential and fundamental. This is to base the house upon the rock. All the edifice of Christian life and consolation is thus made to rest on the ever-faithful Christ, whose words are treasured and obeyed, and whose redeeming grace gives to conscience both peace and liberty. It is one rock for all who are wise. Whatever the diversities in the houses of those who hear and do, all have the same foundation. The illustrious and the obscure, the learned and the unlearned, the courageous and the timid, the wise of every nation and every tribe, build on the same rock, Jesus Christ, the same yesterday, to-day, and for ever.

2. To the latter — the foolish builder — "shall be likened" the disobedient hearer of the words of Christ. He listens and seems to honour and approve, yet does not keep or do the Word—is no true disciple. Alas! how frequent are such builders in every Church! They hear, but do not. They say "Lord, Lord," but give to the Lord neither faith nor obedience. They persist in building up a religious hope and what they take for a religious character, but all the while they are on an uncertain sand, not on the immovable rock.

II. *The day of trial.*

In fair weather the two houses described

may look equally safe, but a day of storm soon tells the difference. The rains descend, soaking both houses from above. The floods come sidelong, washing away the surrounding earth. The winds beat on the naked walls. Then the one house, carefully and strongly founded, bears the strain ; but the other, being " without a foundation," has no grip of the ground, and falls.

Now there are many critical hours in life that test to some extent our spiritual character and hope ; but the day of judgment indicated for the two houses is properly that day of which our Lord had spoken in which doers of His Father's will will be received into the kingdom of heaven, and workers of iniquity, however they may cry " Lord, Lord," will be shut out. Then will all hollow discipleship be exposed, and great will be the fall thereof. Perhaps the germ of the whole illustration lies in the ancient proverb, " The wicked are overthrown, and are not, but the house of the righteous shall stand." *

The higher and larger the foolish builder's

* Proverbs xii. 7.

house, the greater the ruin into which it falls. Disappointment of vain hopes confidently cherished enhances the misery of perdition. Alas! how many such catastrophes there are, and others preparing every hour! It is melancholy enough to survey the desolations that time and war have made upon the earth, broken temples and mouldering palaces, and mere heaps of rubbish where once stood cities powerful and proud. But what is the fall of brick walls or stone columns to the ruined houses of vain hope in human history? Think of men hearing the Word of Christ, and yet through folly and disobedience losing the kingdom of heaven! How great the fall! How piteous the ruin!

With these sad words, " Great was the fall of it," ended the Sermon on the Mount. A mournful cadence truly, which, sinking into the ears and hearts of the audience, surely kept them from trifling with the words of Jesus. Indeed we know that the people were awe-stricken. He taught them as one having authority, and not as the Scribes. And He calmly divided men into two classes, the wise and the foolish, according to their treatment of Him and His Word—the very distinction made in the ancient Psalms and Proverbs between those who feared Jehovah and those who feared Him not. The parable of the wise and foolish virgins afterwards spoken proceeded on the same lines, and indicated that Jesus claimed to be not a prophet only, but more than a prophet.

IX.

THE PHYSICIAN AND HIS PATIENTS.

"But when He heard it, He said, They that are whole have no need of a physician, but they that are sick."—St. Matt. ix. 12.

"And when Jesus heard it, He saith unto them, They that are whole have no need of a physician, but they that are sick. I came not to call the righteous, but sinners."—St. Mark ii. 17.

"And Jesus answering said unto them, They that are whole have no need of a physician, but they that are sick."—St. Luke v. 31.

It strikes us as a strange thing that Jesus Christ should have been openly blamed for His kindness to those who were degraded and despised. We have learned to admire such consideration on the part of good and religious men. We deem them well occupied in trying to raise the fallen and to recover those who have few to care for them. But this way of thinking has come to us through Christianity. The old world into which our Saviour was born knew hardly anything of that tender pity and philanthropy which nowadays we think so becoming. The Pharisees, who were *par excellence* the religious party in Judea, gave alms publicly for their own credit, but had no real compassion. Though the Old Testament might well have taught them to pity the distressed and consider the case of the poor, they were proud and covetous, and centred all their thoughts on themselves and their ceremonial righteousness. It was a fixed notion with them that a righteous man should visit none but righteous men; and so they did not scruple to regard it as a sign of low tastes and sympathies in Jesus of Nazareth that He received publicans and sinners and sat at table with them.

The answer given by our Lord to the Pharisees took the form of metaphor. It was at once a defence of His own conduct and a direction to His followers in all time coming.

I. *A defence*, complete and unanswerable. Our Saviour did not dispute the very unfavourable character imputed to the publicans and sinners. Let them be quite as bad as the

Pharisees thought them, yet this formed no reason for His avoiding them. On the contrary, it was an argument for His visiting them, and expending much of His time and ministry upon them ; for He was a Physician. His very name, Jesus, came from the verb to heal.

Now this was a view of the Lord's character and occupation which had not occurred to the Pharisees. Always intent on building up their own repute for righteousness by means of scrupulous observances, they assumed that the Nazarene also made it His object to pass for a prophet and a righteous man. As they judged, no one could so pass who mingled with publicans and sinners. The association indicated tastes and sympathies which were unworthy of a righteous man. But here was a new idea which changed the whole aspect of the case. He was a Physician; and whither should a physician go but to the houses of the sick ? Nay, if there be cases of peculiarly severe and dangerous illness, there is all the stronger reason for his visits. To go to houses that other men shun is the honourable mark of his profession.

There could be no misunderstanding of the Lord's answer. The Pharisees knew that He did not refer to bodily treatment, and that the publicans and sinners were not "on beds of languishing." There were physicians in the land, some of them Pharisees; but Jesus did not practise like them. He did, indeed, heal many sick folk with a word; and He did much for the medical skill of future generations by breathing into the hearts of men that temper of pity and consideration which is of the moral essence of the healing art. But the defence of Jesus before the Pharisees was evidently that the publicans and sinners were morally and spiritually in an evil case, and that He, being a Physician for the inner man, was not only justified in going to them, but bound to visit them that He might save them from death. Instead of being reproached, He ought to be praised. And He will be praised for ever and ever by those whom He has healed. Oh! kind and thoughtful Saviour! who came not as a Jewish Rabbi, nor as a

Greek philosopher, despising the people, but as a Healer of the sick and Restorer of the faint, and drawing near even to most sinful men, as a physician goes near to his patients to examine each case with patience and apply the necessary cure !

> " Thy kind but searching glance can scan
> The very wounds that shame would hide."

II. *A direction to His followers.*

While our Lord answered the Pharisees, He meant that His disciples should listen and learn. As He was, so should they become in His service. His Church was to be a prolonged expression and an active exponent of healing skill and mercy.

Indeed, in the early Church the care and cure of sick folk formed a recognised part of the duty of Church-officers. Nowadays the physical treatment is assigned to trained physicians and nurses. But whatever be the division of labour, the truth remains that the ministry of healing is eminently Christian, and is part of God's great dispensation of restoring mercy. Still, as with Christ, so with the

Church, the higher ministry is that of moral and spiritual healing; and this is to be taken kindly and freely to the chief of sinners.

1. *Christianity is remedial.*—This consideration should powerfully influence preaching and teaching. To expatiate on the lofty idealism of Christianity, its serene philosophy, and its moral beauty, may be proper in itself and helpful to some minds, but it is not what men at large need most to hear. Before all, let preachers make known its Divine remedy for the fallen, the broken, the perishing. True that Christ is a great Teacher and a great Example; true also that He is the great Revealer of the Father; but what men most urgently require at His hand, and what men troubled in conscience and sore at heart want to learn, is the healing power and saving grace of Christ, the Son and the Messenger of God. They must have their wounds probed, their inward ailment treated, and must be told of Him who "came to seek and to save that which was lost."

This view of Christianity excludes fastidiousness. It may be all very well for men to whom religion is nothing but self-righteousness to keep aloof from sinners for fear of moral contamination; but as a physician is bound to enter chambers of infectious disease in order to heal the body, so must Christianity be taken even into the haunts of vice in order to heal the soul, and bring back the life of conscience and of pure affections. Our religion is not too dainty to "step down into the gutter" and visit great sinners, or so disdainful as to shrink from recognising those men and women whom society disowns. "Its proper vocation is to find the lost, to lift the low, to teach the ignorant, to set free those in bonds, to wash the unclean, to heal the sick; and it must go where it can discover the proper subjects of its art, remembering that the whole need not a physician, but they that are sick." *

Christian Pharisees do not understand this. They wish for churches well appointed and services well performed, in which they and others of similar good repute may go through their devotions at proper times and con-

* Dr. A. B. Bruce, Galilean Gospel, p. 80.

venient seasons; but with aggression on the dominion of evil and the rescue of the perishing they have no real sympathy. They still have need to learn the meaning of that word of God, "I will have mercy and not sacrifice." Indeed, there are very few, if any, Christians who do not need to revolve that saying in their hearts, and more perfectly learn its lesson. It ought to be their most congenial occupation to show to men the Divine mercy, and their unselfish joy to find that the most heinous sinners obtain mercy, that the most vile "are washed and sanctified and justified in the name of the Lord Jesus, and by the Spirit of our God."

2. *Christianity is hopeful.*—It has derived this temper from Christ Himself.

Hopefulness on the part of a physician is not worth much if he is careless in his *diagnosis*, and makes only a hasty and superficial examination of his patient's case. It shows only a sanguine mood. Neither is it of much value when it is only assumed in order to keep up the spirits of the patient. But there is nothing of this sort in what we call the hopefulness of Christ and Christianity. Our Good Physician makes a most serious and accurate *diagnosis* of every case. He knew the sinfulness of those to whom He ministered far more thoroughly than the Pharisees did. Yet, while they gave up the publicans and sinners as incurable, He treated them hopefully, because He knew that grace could save the very worst of them. He actually asserted that publicans and harlots, repenting under the faithful preaching of John the Baptist, went into the kingdom of God before the Scribes and Pharisees.

In the like spirit of hopefulness should the Church look upon mankind, and despair of none. She knows of a sovereign healing balm for even those who are "full of wounds, bruises, and putrefying sores." The power of the Holy Ghost can change the hearts and lives of the most heinous sinners. The blood of Christ can wash all their stains away.

If the Pharisees had thought it of any use to try to elevate the people, they would have attempted the task by insisting on their keeping the law and the traditions of the elders; and they would have failed, because law and tradition have no healing or renewing power. Some of the more austere religious men, as the Essenes, would have enjoined ascetic practices, and would have effected nothing, because imposed austerities do not purify the heart. Christ had a more excellent way, and the secret of it He has transmitted to His Church. It is the way of much love, much hope, much sympathy. He spoke, and His Church should speak, to sinful men of Divine absolution and release from the guilty past; should inspire them with new desires and start them on a new career. Shall our physicians go about the streets visiting the sick, and sparing no pains and no ingenuity to heal them; and shall the Church of God let moral ruin go on unchecked, and men and women grow more and more sick unto death in their souls without an effort to restore them? It must not be. The sin and misery in the world call loudly for the enthusiasm and ingenuity of Christian hope and love ; and they please the Heavenly Physician best who carry the gospel of His salvation to those whom the successors of the Pharisees despair of or disdain.

A physician once told us that he kept himself in health by going to see patients. Whenever he discontinued this, and insisted on patients coming to him, or when he tried to go out of practice altogether, he fell into lethargy, and lost both physical and mental power ; but so soon as he resumed active efforts to heal others, his own health returned. Let servants and handmaids of Christ take the hint. He who desires a sound, strong, spiritual life and health in himself should go and try to heal others, showing patience, sympathy, and hopefulness. This is to walk as Christ walked. And wherever one succeeds, under the blessing of Christ, in converting a sinner from the error of his ways, he " saves a soul from death and hides a multitude of sins."

X.

GARMENTS AND WINE-SKINS.

"And no man putteth a piece of undressed cloth upon an old garment; for that which should fill it up taketh from the garment, and a worse rent is made. Neither do men put new wine into old wine-skins: else the skins burst, and the wine is spilled, and the skins perish: but they put new wine into fresh wine-skins, and both are preserved."—St. Matt. ix. 16, 17.

"No man seweth a piece of undressed cloth on an old garment: else that which should fill it up taketh from it, the new from the old, and a worse rent is made. And no man putteth new wine into old wine-skins; else the wine will burst the skins, and the wine perisheth, and the skins: but they put new wine into fresh wine - skins."— St. Mark ii. 21, 22.

"And He spake also a parable unto them; No man rendeth a piece from a new garment and putteth it upon an old garment; else he will rend the new, and also the piece from the new will not agree with the old. And no man putteth new wine into old wine-skins; else the new wine will burst the skins, and itself will be spilled, and the skins will perish. But new wine must be put into fresh wine-skins. And no man having drunk old wine desireth new: for he saith, The old is good."— St. Luke v. 36-39.

By these illustrations our Lord conveyed a lesson on the charm of naturalness and the law of congruity in religion. Times of transition are critical. The disciples of John the Baptist were anxious to know whether Jesus meant only to reform the old Judaism, or to break away from it and introduce a new faith, with new rules and usages. On the question of fasting, for instance, they agreed with the Pharisees, and were concerned to find that the disciples of Jesus differed. Then the Lord answered them with heavenly metaphors which clothed a grave lesson with a veil of kindly humour.

As old cloth and new cloth are one in being cloth, old wine and new are one in being wine; so the religion before Christ and that which He introduced are essentially one in kind, if not in quality. But it would not answer any good purpose to limit the new by the conditions of the old, or to place the Christian faith and life under the rules of the Pharisees, or even of the disciples of John. So Jesus put it very plainly that He had not come to patch up Pharisaism, or garnish Rabbinism, or to pour His doctrine and all its vital force into the rigid forms of the later Judaism.

Some of the disciples of John had become followers of Jesus. Those who had not, but continued to be known under the former title as a separate party, evidently were suspicious of the new influence. They were anxious for a conservatism which at such a time would have hindered and marred the whole mission of our Saviour. From Him was to date a new era. Under His name and His Spirit was to come a new dispensation of grace and truth. And it would serve no good purpose to attach this to forms or to limit it by restrictions which were incongruous with the genius and liberty of the gospel.

The effect of a forced junction of the old and the new would be injurious to both. This is shown by throwing the illustration of the old garment patched with undressed cloth into two forms. St. Matthew and St. Mark report the Lord as indicating the damage to the old, whilst St. Luke reports Him as pointing out the injury to the new. The first and second Evangelists have it that the undressed cloth would tear away from the old garment, and so make its condition worse than before.

The third Evangelist has it that to take a patch from a new garment and put it on an old one would not make the old one fit to wear, for the one cloth would not agree with the other, while it would incurably spoil the new garment by mangling it. In either case, it will be observed, the disruptive force is in the new. So to make Christianity a mere *addendum* to Rabbinical Judaism would only spoil the former, and would not preserve the latter. The old should be allowed to become antiquated, and the new should be permitted to form its own career.

The second metaphor is to the same effect. To insist on the disciples of Jesus fasting because the Pharisees and the disciples of John fasted by rule, was to repress their joy at a time when they had a right to rejoice, and this was as unwise as to pour new wine into old wine-skins and shut it up. The result would be that the wine, which still needed to work itself clear, would burst the stiff old skins and be spilt. Thus again the Lord taught that a forced amalgamation of the old and the new dispensation would be disastrous to both. Let the law of congruity be observed. Let the new wine be poured into new skins that would yield and not burst; so would both form and substance be preserved.

As for the old wine, our Lord gave no opinion of its value; but with a kindly concession to those whose prejudices He and His disciples had offended, He recognised their preference for the old style of things. Just as on other occasions He conceded to the Pharisees that they were whole, and righteous, and needed no repentance, and then answered them on their own assumption, so here, according to St. Luke's report, He admitted that those who drink the old wine prefer it. It is a difficult thing for minds attached to use and wont to do justice to new movements, especially at the beginning of such movements, when they are like new wine, which still has to outgrow its crudeness, work itself clear of sediment, and acquire its proper flavour. But the Christian life, with its joy and elasticity, could only be understood if taken as a new wine, and therefore it needed

its own forms of development, and was not
to be restricted by the precisianism of the
Pharisees and the disciples of John.

"What 'sweet reasonableness' in the saying of Jesus concerning the old wine and the
new ! . . . What clear insight into the signi-
ficance of His own position and vocation ;
what confidence in His own cause ; what
resolute determination to maintain His inde-
pendence and to decline all stultifying com-
promises ; and yet withal, what patience and
tolerance towards all honest, earnest men who
in matters of religion cannot see with His
eyes ! " *

* Dr. A. Bruce, Parabolic Teaching of Christ, p. 308.

XI.

THE HARVEST AND THE LABOURERS.

"Then saith He unto His disciples, The harvest truly is plenteous, but the labourers are few. Pray ye therefore the Lord of the harvest, that He send forth labourers into His harvest."—St. Matt. ix. 37, 38.

"Say not ye, There are yet four months, and then cometh the harvest? behold, I say unto you, Lift up your eyes, and look on the fields, that they are white already unto harvest. He that reapeth receiveth wages, and gathereth fruit unto life eternal; that he that soweth and he that reapeth may rejoice together. For herein is the saying true, One soweth, and another reapeth. I sent you to reap that whereon ye have not laboured: others have laboured, and ye are entered into their labour."—St. John iv. 35-38.

On the occasion mentioned by St. Matthew, there were fields of ripe corn within sight. We so judge because the time indicated is that of the constituting of the apostolate; and immediately before that event the disciples going through the corn-fields plucked ears and ate them, "rubbing them in their hands.* The corn therefore was ripe. The words reported by St. John were spoken four months earlier, when the fields were comparatively bare. The Lord, therefore, in speaking of a spiritual harvest, pointed to the fields around, in the one instance for a similitude, in the other for a contrast.

In Samaria Jesus recognised, and bade His disciples recognise, fields already white to harvest. He meant that the people were ready to hear if only the gospel were delivered to them. He saw the country opening to His Word, and crowds prepared by their very misery to welcome good tidings of health and peace.

But there was risk of letting the favourable opportunity slip for want of preachers. Now, what can be more vexatious to a farmer than to see a bountiful crop ripe in the fields wasting and spoiling for lack of hands to secure it in season? So grievous was it to Christ to see the leaders of the nation indifferent or hostile to His heavenly message, and better teachers very scarce—the harvest great and the labourers few.

* St. Luke vi. 1, 12, 13.

H

The fields of opportunity are constantly widening, and there is still no small difficulty about an adequate supply of labourers. Home fields are scrambled over, and while there are too many labourers in some corners, other spots are neglected. In foreign fields, labourers are much too far apart, and their strength is often sorely overtaxed. It is easy enough to multiply ecclesiastics, but labourers together with God, workmen that need not be ashamed, have always been too few for the harvest - field. And field-work needs labouring men. Especially when the crop ripens, time is precious, and the reapers must not spare themselves who would gather the corn in its season.

Labourers such as ' Jesus Christ desiderated are all the better of a training as well as a will to work. In every kind of human activity training tells. Sustained and thorough work of a high class cannot be had without it. And we find that our Lord was at great pains with the training of the twelve. But the first requisite for labourers is that they be sent to the work by the Lord of the harvest. And the Church must pray continually to have such labourers sent, and that with a certain force of conviction and pressure of conscience bearing them over scruples and fears, and compelling them to preach the gospel.

While Jesus was on earth in the form of a servant, the Father in heaven was Lord of the harvest. Therefore He prayed to the Father the whole night through before He called and commissioned the twelve; and we must hope that the disciples, in obedience to His word, also prayed to the Father on that night to send out labourers. In the morning the prayer was answered in the selection and mission of the twelve apostles.

Now that Jesus has ascended, and is Lord and Head of the Church, and over all things to the Church, it is right to regard and invoke Him as Lord of the harvest; for His is the gift of labourers. "He has given some to be apostles, and some prophets, and some evangelists, and some pastors and teachers." *

* Eph. iv. 11.

The question, perhaps, suggests itself—
"Why are we required to solicit the Lord
of the harvest on such a point as this?"
The fields are His, and He must know the
value of opportunity and the need of
labourers far better than we. Surely He
will of His own accord provide labourers.
But it is a mistake to suppose that prayer
is enjoined in order to tell the Lord what
He does not know, or to persuade Him to
do what He might otherwise neglect. A
great object of it is to bring the hearts of
His followers into harmony with the will of
Christ and of God. So in the matter of
harvest-work, our Lord wished His disciples
to be in unison with Himself and with the
Father in heaven on the great and urgent
task of preaching the gospel and saving the
people. He would have them desire what
He already desired. It is the same thing
still. The Church praying for missionaries
is praying according to the will of God. The
petition, "Thy kingdom come!" is well followed by "Thy will be done!"

"He that reapeth receiveth wages." All

honest humble labour in the field shall have gracious reward at the Lord's appearing. "They that turn many to righteousness shall shine as the stars for ever and ever."

XII.

SERPENTS AND DOVES.

"Behold, I send you forth as sheep in the midst of wolves: be ye therefore wise as serpents, and harmless as doves."

—St. Matt. x. 16.

THE apostles of Christ, when persecuted, were not to attempt to meet force by force of the same description. They could no more fight their enemies than sheep can fight a pack of wolves. They were to be defenceless, as their Master was, against the malice of those who hated them. And as He was put to death by cruel men, who compassed Him about as so many wild dogs, so also would some of them be. Yet the result of the conflict was to be in favour of the "little flock." The weak were to confound the mighty; the sheep were to keep the wolves at bay; for there is a Divine Keeper of the sheep who knows how to lay restraint on enemies of His flock, and to give the conquest to the weak. The meek endurance of the apostles and other messengers of Christ was to win a signal victory.

By a double reference to the serpents and the doves of Palestine, the Lord indicated to His apostles the spirit in which they ought to meet hardship and violence. They should combine the wariness of serpents in respect of danger with the guilelessness of doves. It is a blending of qualities, a balancing and harmonising of apparent opposites, which no one attains to without pains and prayer. The men of Galilee who were going out under their first apostolic mission were not by any means as yet up to this standard. The Master said to them, "Become ye prudent as the serpents, but unwily as the doves." The servants of Christ should be, on the one hand, wary, but not crafty; on the other, simple, but not simpletons.

I. "*Wary as the serpents.*"
The illustration must be confined to the one

point which is indicated.   He who on another occasion stigmatised the hypocritical Scribes and Pharisees as " serpents " and " the off-spring of vipers " * was not likely to bid His apostles be " as serpents."   He spoke of serpentlike prudence evidently with an exclusive reference to the shrewd instinct by which those creatures perceive impending danger and avoid it.   His apostles ought not to offer themselves to injury or martyrdom, or involve themselves needlessly in trouble or danger.   They were bound to use discretion, and even astuteness, in avoiding mischief and guarding life and liberty.

"Beware of men" is the counsel which immediately follows.   If the apostles found themselves involved in danger and arraigned " before governors and kings," they were not to fear, but speak out as " the Spirit of the Father" would guide and embolden them to do ; but if they could foresee, and with a good conscience avoid, such peril, self-preservation was not to be despised as pusillanimity, but to be attended to as a reasonable duty.

* St. Matt. xxiii. 33.

It may be supposed that men hardly need exhortation to take care of themselves; but in point of fact men do need such admonition when they are carried away by a strong enthusiasm. It is a familiar incident in war that young soldiers, ardent and burning for distinction, foolishly and unnecessarily expose themselves, and are with difficulty restrained. Something like this appeared in the Church of Christ after a generation or two had passed. There arose a fanatical thirst for martyrdom, stimulated by the excessive honour which had come to be paid to the names and relics of the slain confessors of Christ. But this was a departure from the example and teaching of the Saviour Himself and of His apostles. He avoided capture by His enemies till the set time appointed by the Father for His being offered up at Jerusalem. He directed His disciples, when they should be persecuted in one city, to flee to another. And instances of the avoidance of danger are obvious in the Acts of the Apostles. When Paul and Barnabas "were ware," or became aware, of an intention to assault them at Iconium, they did well to flee to the cities of Lycaonia. When the former of them was at Ephesus, and a great tumult was stirred up in defence of the worship of Diana, the brethren did well who kept him back from gratuitous exposure to danger. They suffered him not to "enter in unto the people." And the Asiarchs who were his judicious friends desired him not to "adventure himself into the theatre." The same Apostle, as brave a spirit as ever lived, repeatedly showed in time of danger his obedience to the Lord's word in favour of wariness. He skilfully hushed an angry mob at Jerusalem by turning from the Greek language in which he had spoken to the Roman commandant, and addressing the crowd in the Hebrew tongue. With similar astuteness, he cast discord among his enemies in the Jewish Council, rousing the Pharisees against the Sadducees, till the din brought the guard of soldiers to his rescue.

It is enough to indicate the kind of prudence which our Lord enjoined. Particular cases in which it should be exercised must be judged of one by one as they occur. The general principle is that a servant of Christ should not court reproach, invite trouble, or involve himself in suffering or in danger, if he may honourably and conscientiously avoid it. And by inference we get a similar direction for active service. Zeal is good, but if not associated with tact and discretion, it may do harm by provoking irritation against the truth and exposing holy things to contempt.

No doubt there is difficulty on either side; and a good man trying to keep the balance between the extremes of caution and rashness may easily be misconstrued. When he is bold, he may be represented as forward and vain-glorious. When he is guarded, he may be stigmatised as selfish and designing. It is evident that St. Paul was blamed by some for boldness, and by others for duplicity; and indeed it is no bad sign of any Christian man that he is accused of opposite faults, and from opposite directions. Every servant of the Lord who is of any public use has to run the gauntlet of censure, and have darts thrown at him from opposite sides. If he is valiant for the truth, there are always some to call him forward, intolerant, controversial, fussy, perhaps a little crazy. If he is discreet, there are those who put him down at once as a knowing fellow, who plays his cards shrewdly in religion, and studies his own interest.

The good man need not be greatly disturbed by such unjust imputations, so long as he has the testimony of a pure conscience. At the same time he may learn something even from unfair reproach. He may see in what respects his conduct may lie open to question, and his good may be "evil spoken of." He may perceive how necessary it is to exercise caution and prudence so as to preclude offence, if that be possible, and raise no obstacles to his own usefulness of a kind that a little forethought and self-control might have obviated. He who becomes wise as the serpent will avoid not only serious dangers, but also those blunders in manner and breaches of temper which hinder much good.

II. "*And guileless as the doves.*"
No doubt the word "harmless" has an

appropriate meaning, for the apostles were to suffer wrong, not to inflict it. But such is the idea conveyed in the figure of unresisting sheep surrounded by wolves. The characteristic of the dove intended by Christ was evidently meant to balance the knowingness of the serpent. And this is the unwiliness of that bird—the figure of a pure and ingenuous nature. So the apostles of Christ, while behaving themselves prudently, were to ignore wiles and stratagems, and pursue their ministry with a holy frankness and simplicity. They might often seem to throw themselves at the mercy of those who would fly at them as hawks at turtledoves. Yet the innocent doves would defeat the hawks, as the sheep were to overcome the wolves. Blessed are the meek.

The Lord Jesus is the consummate example to illustrate His own teaching. He was always on His guard, and penetrated all the manœuvres and plots of those who watched and hated Him. He fell into none of their snares; never lost self-possession; never spoke at random; uttered all His words and conducted all His intercourse with infinite discretion.

But He formed no counterplots and devised no stratagems. No craft was in His bosom; no guile was in His mouth. Everywhere He showed that the Spirit which rested upon Him had descended in the form of a dove.

So let our wisdom be meekness of wisdom. Be not all serpent, subtle serpent! Be not all dove, silly dove!

XIII.

CHILDREN AT PLAY.

"But whereunto shall I liken this generation? It is like unto children sitting in the market-places, which call unto their fellows, and say, We piped unto you, and ye did not dance ; we wailed, and ye did not mourn. For John came neither eating nor drinking, and they say, He hath a devil. The Son of Man came eating and drinking, and they say, Behold, a gluttonous man, and a wine-bibber, a friend of publicans and sinners ! And wisdom is justified by her works."—ST. MATT. xi. 16-19.

"Whereunto then shall I liken the men of this generation, and to what are they like? They are like unto children that sit in the market-place, and call one to another; which say, We piped unto you, and ye did not dance ; we wailed, and ye did not weep. For John the Baptist is come eating no bread nor drinking wine; and ye say, He hath a devil. The Son of Man is come eating and drinking ; and ye say, Behold a gluttonous man, and a wine-bibber, a friend of publicans and sinners ! "—ST. LUKE vii. 31-34.

THE difference between John the Baptist and Jesus Christ was laid hold of by unfriendly minds to justify their non-reception of the Saviour : whereupon He showed that their bearing alike toward His forerunner and toward Himself had been childish and petulant. The ascetic life of John had offended them

on the one hand; the gracious social deport-
ment of Jesus offended them on the other.

To give point to this statement He introduced an illustration which might never have
occurred to a solitary like John, but was quite
natural in the lips of Jesus, who had lived in
towns, and was accustomed to pass through
streets and market-places. With the interest
and sympathy that belonged to His genuine
human heart, He had observed the sports of
children in their noisy glee. So He pictured
a group of little children playing at *make-
believe* marriages and funerals. First they
acted a marriage procession; some of them
piping as on instruments of music, while the
rest were expected to leap and dance. In a
perverse mood, however, these last did not
respond, but stood still and looked discontented. So the little pipers changed their
game and proposed a funeral. They began to
imitate the loud wailing of Eastern mourners.
But again they were thwarted, for their companions refused to chime in with the mournful cry and to beat their breasts. Neither
the one game nor the other suited their

petulant spirit. So the disappointed children who had struck up the wedding-march and then changed it for the funeral wail complained, "We piped unto you, and ye did not dance; we wailed, and ye did not mourn." "Nothing pleases you. If you don't want to dance, why don't you mourn? Or, if you don't like the funeral play, why did you refuse the marriage? It is plain that you are in bad humour, and determined not to be pleased."

So was it with the generation which surrounded our Saviour. They refused John the Baptist because he was too austere, and then refused Jesus under the pretext that He was not austere enough. It was evident that they judged and acted, not on grounds of reason, but on mere caprice and prejudice.

It was spoken in pleasant fashion, but it was a sharp rebuke. It is well to be as children in simplicity, but not at all well to be like them in mere petulance and folly. A childish person is one whose moral judgment is worth little, and whose character evolves no moral force. A childish generation must be in its dotage, and its opinions have no title to respect.

The games of the children in this similitude were so selected as to suggest the contrast between the Saviour and the Baptist. But in the history the more severe ministry went first, and that which was genial and gracious followed. First appeared John, a dweller in solitudes, holding himself aloof from the domestic and social life of his countrymen, clothed with the power and animated by the spirit of the prophet Elijah. He was seen in his dress of camel's hair, with sad countenance, inveighing against the evils of the time, and summoning men of all orders and classes to repentance. At the tables of other men he was not seen. He "came neither eating nor drinking," for he found enough in the desert for his simple wants. Such a man and such a ministry ought to have made a profound impression on a people who gloried in the memory of those prophets of the desert, Moses and Elijah. And for a little while John seemed to have a great success. Multitudes took him for a prophet, and repaired to him for baptism. A certain number attached themselves closely to him as his disciples; but these appear to have been uninfluential Galileans, like the disciples of Jesus. The rulers made some inquiry as to the claim of John to be a prophet, but came to no conclusion, and never were baptized. Then they began to speak against him, professing to regard his austerity as indicative of a disordered brain or of demonic possession. In all times and countries, self-indulgent people are disposed to set down any one whose manner of life tacitly reproves their own as "a bit of a fanatic," or as more or less crazy.

Still, the rulers would, at all events, have been consistent with themselves if they had adhered to the view that austerity is demonic rather than divine. But their behaviour to Jesus of Nazareth showed that they proceeded in their judgment on no consistent principle, but on suggestions of prejudice and malice. The Son of Man entered the houses of men and sat at their tables. Freely He mixed with home life, and was both accessible and sympathetic.   He preached repentance, not in the deserts, but in houses and in the streets. And lo! the rulers, who had disdained the desert preacher as a demoniac, reviled the street and house preacher as lax and given to pampering the flesh.   Neither tone of character, neither mode of ministry, could find favour, or even win fair play, from that perverse generation.

This sort of unreason shows itself again and again.   Men will find fault with Christ and Christianity, put the matter how you will.   The doctrine is too high or not high enough.   The precepts are too austere or too indefinite.   The gospel is too hard or too easy.   Prejudice can always find some objection; and proud men who do not like John because he preaches repentance, do not like Jesus because He not only preaches repentance, but brings gratuitous salvation to the heart and to the home.

The attitude of Christians toward society is not seldom made a ground of censure by persons who have a good deal in common with the Pharisees and rulers of the Jews.

They are too unsocial or they are too social. The critics are hard to please. If a Christian be reserved in his habits and a lover of retirement, they describe him as narrow and ungenial. If he be frank and accessible, they shake their heads over his worldliness and inordinate love of society. He is never quite right in their eyes. He is too strict or too yielding ; too gloomy or too happy ; too cautious or too bold ; too shrewd or too simple. Let not such judgments of men disconcert or discourage any who with an honest heart endeavour to be true to Christ. The Lord Himself is our Master and our Example. Therefore we do right to enter the houses and sit at the tables of our friends when they invite us. But there and everywhere we are to bear ourselves as becomes His disciples. How far we may mingle with those who are the modern representatives of "the publicans and sinners" is a question of discretion. What is safe for very decided Christians may be imprudent in those who are less experienced. What carries little risk to those of full age may be very dan-

gerous for the young. We may draw near
to the classes of persons alluded to (and they
are by no means confined to the lowest social
ranks), if one can do so after the manner of
Christ, not to be partakers of other men's
sins or to countenance their excess, but to
turn them from their sins and win them
back to God. All the while we must be on
our guard against the contamination of our
own imaginations and hearts, for we have not
that perfect inward purity of Christ, which
could no more be sullied by proximity to the
publicans and sinners than the daylight is
soiled by glancing on refuse and corruption.

XIV.

BAD LEAVEN.

"And Jesus said unto them, Take heed and beware of the leaven of the Pharisees and Sadducees. . . . Then understood they how that he bade them not beware of the leaven of bread, but of the teaching of the Pharisees and Sadducees."—St. Matt. xvi. 6, 12.

"And he charged them, saying, Take heed, beware of the leaven of the Pharisees and the leaven of Herod."—St. Mark. viii. 15.

"He began to say unto His disciples first of all, Beware ye of the leaven of the Pharisees, which is hypocrisy."—St. Luke xii. 1.

However hostile to each other, the Pharisees and Sadducees made common cause against Jesus Christ. He encountered them even in remote corners of the land. For example, on the occasion of a visit which He paid to "the borders of Magadan," or parts of Dalmanutha, members of both these sects accosted Him so soon as He landed from the boat, and called His prophetic mission in question by demanding of Him "a sign from heaven." At once He detected the unfriendly and un- reasonable temper which actuated the demand; so He refused it, and re-embarking, departed out of their coasts. St. Mark adds the graphic and pathetic touch that our Lord "sighed deeply in His spirit."

He recrossed the lake, the disciples, as usual, managing the boat. Apparently He was silent on the way, musing in sorrow on the indisposition shown by Pharisees and Sad- ducees even in a rural district far from the headquarters of those sects at Jerusalem. The whole country was pervaded by their influ- ence. At last He broke silence with this charge to His disciples, "Take heed, and beware of the leaven of the Pharisees and Sadducees!" The apostles were perplexed. Their thoughts had not been running in the same groove with His. If they had been reflecting on what had happened at Dalmanutha, not improbably they had regretted that their Master did not satisfy the demand of those who met Him, and that He so quickly and abruptly turned away. He was sorrowful because those people of

Dalmanutha had craved of Him "a sign from heaven." The disciples were disappointed that He had not shown some celestial sign or prodigy, and so silenced the gainsayers. Thus, at cross purposes with Him, they were not quick to catch His meaning. They fell on a prosaic and almost paltry explanation of His metaphor, supposing that the Master referred to their having omitted to take a supply of bread with them for the little voyage; and thus they added yet another to the list of blunders and misconceptions with which they tried the patience of the Lord Jesus.

To understand the surmise of the disciples, one must bear in mind the scruples of Jewish casuistry regarding the lawfulness of taking leaven from certain parties. Dr. John Lightfoot has shown that Rabbinical teachers gravely discussed the question whether leaven for baking bread might be accepted from a heathen, and suggests that the disciples on this occasion supposed their Master to be laying down a regulation against the taking of household baking-leaven from a Pharisee or a Sadducee.*

* *Horæ Hebraicæ, in loco.*

But on the lips of Jesus leaven was a metaphor. He meant that His disciples should beware of the teaching of these sects. The point of analogy is the self-diffusing power of any doctrine that accords with the self-righteous and self-pleasing tendencies of human nature. Such teaching by the Pharisees and Sadducees had spread through the community, just as leaven might spread through a mass of dough. Let the disciples look to it that they themselves should not come under the influence of this evil leaven !

It is important to the interpretation to notice that although, according to the various accounts, our Lord spoke of three sects, He ascribed to them one and the same leaven. From this it is obvious that His reference was not so much to the distinctive tenets of the sects as to a way of thinking and judging which was common to them all, and especially their mode of testing His Divine mission by a demand for signs from heaven. The leaven of the Pharisees was hypocrisy. They were the conventional, traditional, and ritualistic party. Zealots for the law and the oral traditions, which interpreted and supplemented the law, they were incensed against the unconventional and heart-searching ministry of Jesus; and their implied offer to believe in Him, provided that He would work such a prodigy as they demanded, was but a hollow pretext. The Sadducees were the rationalistic party of the period, and were of a worldly and self-pleasing temper. For those cold sceptics to ask a sign from heaven was an arrant piece of hypocrisy. With them the Herodians seem to be joined, either because the Galilean Sadducees were prominent adherents of the shallow, pleasure-loving Tetrarch, or because Herod himself was a Sadducee.

The bearing of all those sects towards Jesus of Nazareth was insincere and heartless. They were restive under His word, so pure, so fresh, so divinely simple: so they combined to dispute His claims and resist His growing influence. And this way of thinking and judging spread from them to many who were not of the sects, making the ministry of Jesus increasingly difficult. It worked like leaven ; and the apostles themselves were liable to be infected by it if they did not beware.

One may see that wherever Jesus Christ goes in this world, the Pharisees and Sadducees come forth to meet Him, and do what they can to drive Him away. The tendencies which those sects exhibited in Judea and Galilee are in human nature, and re-appear in the religious history of every people.

There is always a party of ostentatious strictness, of elaborate regulations and ceremonial rigour. And of the same school, though they may loudly disclaim it, are many vehement anti-ritualists, who are far too conscious of their own superior type of piety, and despise others. All those Pharisees have a certain hardness and pedantry of judgment, and are quite out of sympathy with the Divine "love to the world." It is a repellant pragmatical style of religiousness, intensely opposed to the mind of Christ.

There is always a party of rationalists, and with them are those who think that religion ought to be regulated by the State— a sort of modern Herodians. These Saddu- cees do not propose to dispense with faith altogether, but they are always anxious that it should not "go too far." Their idea is to let the supernatural element disperse in thin vapour, and to be content with a moral system elegantly embellished with high sen- timents, and not too severe in its exactions. This way of thinking, working as it does equally with Pharisaism against the gospel, has the same leaven; and it spreads not so much by any argument or intellectual per- suasion, as by a sort of contagion, taking hold of the minds that are naturally predisposed either to self-pleasing rigour or to self-pleasing laxity.

Our Saviour gave place to those sectaries no, not a hair's breadth. He would not gra- tify their demand for a sign, or in any degree diverge from His appointed path to conciliate them. And this is all the more remarkable when we consider how accessible He was to inquirers and petitioners of all ranks, how kind to the populace, and how patient with

His own blundering and questioning disciples. There was reason for it. The demand for a sign from heaven betrayed a temper of mind which could not and should not be satisfied. It implied that all the proofs of His Divine mission already given by words of truth and works of healing were doubtful or inadequate, and that He might be required to play the magician at every place which He visited in order to convince His opponents that He was a man sent from God. To yield to such a demand would have been to put a premium on obstinate unbelief.

Christians ought in this to learn of Christ. There are demands for evidence which should not be heeded. A temper of prejudice and antipathy is not to be humoured. Beware of the bad leaven ! There are evidences enough to satisfy a candid mind. And those who, in sympathy with Jesus, are bent on doing the Father's will, know quite well that His doctrine is from God.

It is a significant fact that the Pharisees and Sadducees could not let Jesus alone. If the one sect was sure of its legal righteousness, and the other of its worldly-wise rationalism, surely they might have left the Nazarene and His followers in peace. But they were not so sure as they affected to be; they were not at rest, and so they were inquisitive about every symptom of a new religious movement. One sees this in the fact that they went to John's baptism; on which occasion they heard a startling exclamation from that fearless preacher. "O offspring of vipers, who warned you to flee from the wrath to come?" The Saviour felt the same moral repugnance. He had come to abase the proud and exalt the lowly; and between Him and those upholders of their own righteousness and their own wisdom there could be no mutual understanding or concord. And as it was then, so is it still. The Pharisaism and Sadducecism which so largely leaven society are incompatible with Christ and the gospel. They have a fatal power of driving the Saviour away, and making Him "sigh deeply in His spirit."

XV.

THE CHURCH ROCK.

" And I also say unto thee, that thou art Peter, and upon this rock I will build my Church ; and the gates of Hades shall not prevail against it."—St. Matt. xvi. 18.

" Thou art *Petros,* and on this *petra* I will build my Church." The French version of Ostervald loses the play of words by making them identical. " Tu es Pierre, et sur cette pierre," &c. The phrase has been turned over and over in controversy, and made to appear full of difficulty ; but in reality the metaphor is not at all obscure.

Take together all those passages of Scripture which refer to the Church as a holy temple, and to its foundation-stone, and you will find that they fall into two classes. Virtually the same illustration is used in both, but it is differently applied.

In one class of Scriptures, God is the builder

of the Church, and Christ is its corner-stone and sure foundation. If at Corinth St. Paul "as a wise master-builder laid a foundation," he did so simply by making known the risen Saviour; for, as he was careful to explain, "other foundation can no man lay than that which is laid, which is Jesus Christ." * This is truth most precious to the believing heart, and it is the desire to make this all-prominent which has led so many to insist that our Lord, in using the word *petra*, must have pointed to Himself. But the simple fact is that the way of using the metaphor was different.

In the second class of passages, of which Christ's word to St. Peter is the chief instance, our Lord is Himself the builder, and the apostles as witnesses to Him form the foundation or first row of stones, on which all the living stones of the Church are "built together." Thus is avoided the awkwardness of describing our Lord as both the builder and the foundation of the same edifice. And it was very natural that under this use of the

---

* 1 Cor. iii. 9–11. See also Ps. cxviii. 22, 23 ; 1 Pet. ii. 4–6.

metaphor the Great Builder should begin with Simon Peter, who was the foremost of the apostolic band, and had just confessed Jesus to be " the Christ, the Son of the living God." Such a confessor was the very stone of witness needed in the foundation. With him were laid his co-witnesses, the other apostles ; and to them were added the prophets, as also bearing testimony to the Lord.* Let it be remembered that the Church is here regarded mainly as the institution of living and perpetual testimony to Jesus Christ. Its stones are all stones of witness, and therefore the foundation consists of the apostolic and prophetic witnesses. We speak of fundamental articles of faith, but first come fundamental men of faith, and on them and their testimony rest the successive layers of living stones in the Church, *i.e.*, successive generations of men confessing with their mouths and believing in their hearts that God raised Jesus Christ from the dead.

Such is the Church which has the promise of perpetuity. The building is impregnable

* Eph. ii. 20 ; Acts x. 42, 43 ; 1 Cor. xii. 28.

and imperishable. The gates or powers of Hades shall not prevail against it. Christ, the Builder of the Church, keeps those powers under control, for He has " the keys of Hades and of death."[*]

Thus viewing the two ways in which the metaphor of a Church-building is cast, we feel no difficulty with the Lord's language to Simon Peter. It was spoken amidst scenery which strongly suggested the illustration. The country round Cæsarea Philippi is full of rocky cliffs, from which were cut large foundation-stones for temples devoted probably to the worship of Baal. Some of these are still to be seen lying in tiers—single blocks of stone being upwards of twelve feet thick and upwards of sixty feet long.[†] Our Lord very probably spoke with some of those temple foundation-rocks close at hand, and, with His wonted ease of illustration, took

[*] Rev. i. 18.

[†] Dr. Thomson mentions one block in those parts which had never been moved from the quarry. " It is fourteen by seventeen, and sixty-nine feet long."—*The Land and the Book*, chap. xvi.

occasion to speak of the *petra* on which His Church would rest.

We have alluded to the keen controversy which has been waged over this saying of Christ. This is the inscription which glitters in letters of vast dimensions over the interior of the dome of St. Peter's at Rome; and everywhere this is cited by teachers and disputers of the Latin Church to prove the permanent and universal primacy of St. Peter and his alleged successors in the Roman See. Yet any one may see that the words spoken at Cæsarea Philippi make no reference to Rome, and that to use them in support of a Papacy needs not a little controversial audacity. Without entering on the subject at length, we may set down three propositions :—

1. The position of Simon Peter in the foundation of the Church was not an exclusive one, but was shared by the other apostles.* He was the first stone, as he always ranks first in the lists of the apostles, but his colleagues and co-witnesses were in the same

* Eph. ii. 20 ; Rev. xxi. 14.

tier of stones of witness, and made it complete.

2. His honoured position in the foundation and beginning of the Church implied nothing of primacy or popedom, and conveyed no authority to govern the Church in all time coming. The disciples certainly drew no such inference, else how could James and John after this have aspired to the highest seats? Or, when their desire was made known to the Master, how could He have failed to inform them that the chief place was already assigned to Simon Peter and his ecclesiastical successors? How could He have spoken of "twelve thrones" for the twelve apostles, if all were to be subject to the episcopal throne of Peter? Or how could Paul set it down as a mark of sectarianism at Corinth for any to say that they were "of Cephas?"* If the Roman claim is good, it is a mark of Catholicity to be of Cephas. It should be added that from the Book of Acts and his two Epistles we derive a considerable amount of authentic information regarding the work

* 1 Cor. i. 12.

and teaching of St. Peter in the early Church, but we have not the least hint that he exercised the authority of a Pope, or even a Primate. We have many proofs that he did not.*

3. Whatever may have been the importance of St. Peter's position, there is no mention of his successors, least of all of successors at Rome, a city which is connected with St. Paul, and not with St. Peter, in the New Testament. Even though he had been the exclusive foundation-rock of the Church, it would by no means follow that a succession of Roman bishops should be foundations. It is an odd idea of a building proceeding through many centuries, that its base should not be imbedded in the historical past beneath, but should be laid all the way up to the roof. And it is more than odd, it is preposterous, to turn the claim of a continuous foundation into the right of a continuous absolute government.

Yet on such outrageous assumptions rests

* For a clear and compact statement of this, see Dean Howson's *Horæ Petrinæ*, chap. viii.

the loudly-asserted right of the Pope of Rome to rule the whole Church from the chair of Peter, and as vicar of Christ on earth! Few things are so discreditable to the human mind as the success which has attended, and still attends, this egregious imposture.

XVI.

THE KEYS.

" I will give unto thee the keys of the kingdom of heaven :
and whatsoever thou shalt bind on earth shall be bound in heaven :
and whatsoever thou shalt loose on earth shall be loosed in heaven."
—St. Matt. xvi. 19.

WHILE our Lord Jesus Christ, on rising from
the dead, would retain in His own hand " the
keys of Hades and death," He would give to
Simon Peter " the keys of the kingdom of
heaven."

*The kingdom of heaven does not mean
heaven.* Yet the failure to mark this obvious
distinction has given prevalence to the foolish
notion that St. Peter is porter at heaven's
gate, and admits souls to Paradise. Byron
writes it in sarcasm—

" Saint Peter sat by the celestial gate."

But it has been the serious belief of superstitious millions, whose anxiety has been as

to whether St. Peter would admit them to a seat in heaven.

The kingdom of heaven does not mean the Church. It is the dispensation of grace and truth on earth, announced by John the Baptist and inaugurated by Jesus Christ. Under this dispensation and kingdom the Church is being gathered, but it is not accurate to transfer to the latter as an institution what is predicated of the former. Attention to this distinction would have made short work with the Papal claim to the power of the keys, and would have saved our Protestant divines a great deal of discussion regarding the power of the keys in the Church, and the hands in which that power is vested.

But what is meant by the keys? A very child must know that the Lord did not mean to give to the Apostle an actual bunch of keys. The phrase is metaphorical; and the meaning is to be found by comparison of this with other Scriptures. It certainly indicates power, and, as it appears to us, power of two kinds :—(1.) Administrative; and (2.) Didactic.

I. *Administrative.*

The keys of a palace are intrusted to the *major-domo.* The key of the house of David is said in Isaiah to be laid on the shoulders of Eliakim, a trusty counsellor.* The mention of keys suggests stewardship, not lordship. So a power of administration in the kingdom of heaven was assigned to Simon Peter, as the first of the apostles. It is from this that divines have described the right to exercise Church discipline as " the power of the keys," distinguishing it from the jurisdiction of civil rulers, which is enforced by the power of the sword.†

II. *Didactic.*

Jesus reproached the lawyers of the time for having "taken away the key of knowledge."‡ They hindered the enlightenment of their nation. On the other hand, a Scribe well instructed unto the kingdom of heaven had been likened by Him to a householder

---

* Isa. xxii. 20–22.
† Westminster Confession, chap. xxx. 2.
‡ St. Luke xi. 52.

with command of a treasury. We infer that
the Lord promised to Simon Peter the keys
by which he would have access to the treasure
of wisdom and understanding in the kingdom
of heaven, and so be able to teach with clearness and authority.

This interpretation is confirmed by the
words which follow—"And whatsoever thou
shalt bind on earth shall be bound in heaven,
and whatsoever thou shalt loose on earth shall
be loosed in heaven." * Not whomsoever, but
whatsoever. The saying refers to points of
doctrine or practice which might come into
dispute. Among the Jewish Rabbis, to bind
meant to forbid or declare forbidden ; to
loose, meant to allow or declare allowed. We
understand, therefore, that the apostles were
authorised to teach and guide their fellow-
Christians, showing what things were forbidden and what allowed, indicating what
rites and ordinances were superseded, and
how debatable questions should be settled
in the new community. In fact, the power

* This prerogative was shared by all the apostles. See St.
Matt. xviii. 18.

to bind and loose was just the function of directing the judgment and practice of the new-born inexperienced Church, and ordering its beginnings of thought and life according to the mind of Christ.

But while he shared the power to bind and loose with all his colleagues, there is, in the Acts of the Apostles, a very special ascription of the power of the keys to Simon Peter. True, as the "Te Deum" has it, that when our Lord "had overcome the sharpness of death," He "opened the kingdom of heaven to all believers;" but the actual opening of the kingdom was effected through His steward. The door of faith was opened first to the Jews at Jerusalem; * next to the Samaritans, a kind of intermediate people; † and finally to the Gentiles. ‡ So was the gospel given to the whole world; and in each instance it was the hand of Simon Peter that held and turned the key.

* Acts ii. iii. iv.　　† Acts viii.　　‡ Acts x.

XVII.

A LITTLE CHILD.

"In that hour came the disciples unto Jesus, saying, Who then is greatest in the kingdom of heaven? And He called to Him a little child, and set him in the midst of them, and said, Verily, I say unto you, Except ye turn, and become as little children, ye shall in no wise enter into the kingdom of heaven. Whosoever therefore shall humble himself as this little child, the same is the greatest in the kingdom of heaven. And whoso shall receive one such little child in My name receiveth Me: but whoso shall cause one of these little ones which believe on Me to stumble, it is profitable for him that a great millstone should be hanged about his neck, and that he should be sunk in the depth of the sea. . . . See that ye despise not one of these little ones; for I say unto you, that in heaven their angels do always behold the face of My Father which is in heaven. How think ye? If any man have a hundred sheep, and one of them be gone

"And He sat down, and called the twelve; and He saith unto them, If any man would be first, he shall be last of all, and minister of all. And He took a little child, and set him in the midst of them: and taking him in His arms, He said unto them, Whosoever shall receive one of such little children in my name, receiveth Me: and whosoever receiveth Me, receiveth not Me, but Him that sent Me."—St. Mark ix. 35-37.

astray, doth he not leave the
ninety and nine, and go unto the
mountains, and seek that which
goeth astray? And if so be that
he find it, verily I say unto you,
he rejoiceth over it more than
over the ninety and nine which
have not gone astray. Even so
it is not the will of your Father
which is in heaven, that one of
these little ones should perish."
—St. Matt. xviii. 1–6, 10–14.

Jesus Christ loved children, and often referred to them in His teaching. On the occasion now under our notice, He actually called a little child to Him, and by help of the child, a visible and not a merely verbal metaphor, inculcated humility and conveyed consolation to the humble.

I. *Lessons of humility.*

1. A lesson from the child in the midst of the apostles.

The twelve chosen men were but men at the best. They had the same craving for preferment and desire to occupy chief seats that lurks in almost every breast. It was not enough that they should be princes or counsellors in their Master's kingdom. The question which of them should be the greatest fretted their

spirits, and led to an unseemly dispute.
The recent glory of the Transfiguration excited
them as an apparent beginning of their
Messiah's kingdom. Were the three whom
He had taken with Him to "the Holy
Mount" to be promoted permanently above
their colleagues? They knew that the prophets on the mountain had spoken of "the
decease to be accomplished at Jerusalem;"
they had heard solemn words on the same
prospective event from their Master's lips;
but they put away the unwelcome topic,
and would speak only of the kingdom and
the chief places about the King.

This was on the journey from Mount Hermon
to Capernaum; and when the little band had
entered the town, the apostles submitted their
question to the Lord. St. Mark says that He
drew it from them by inquiring after the
subject discussed by them on the way.

His treatment of the matter was marked,
both in matter and manner, by His unfailing
originality. He called to Him a little child—
no doubt a child of the house in which He
rested—and, without fear or hesitation, the

little one came to Him. It is a pleasant incidental proof that there was no austerity in the aspect or bearing of Jesus, such as would make children shrink from or avoid Him. Little ones have a quick and true perception of those who love them; and the child at Capernaum knew at once that the voice which called him was that of a friend.

Then the Lord placed him in the midst of the disciples, and bade those grown men look on that babe and try to be like him. Only by childlikeness could they excel. Indeed, no otherwise could they so much as enter the kingdom of heaven.

At Jerusalem our Lord had taught Nicodemus the Pharisee that he must be born again in order to see the kingdom of God. Now at Capernaum He taught the twelve that, though they were called to be His disciples, they were disqualifying themselves for His kingdom by their temper of jealous rivalry. "Except ye turn," *i.e.*, from the question which of you shall be greater than the rest, and from the spirit which dictates such questions, "and become as little children," ye can have no place at all in the heavenly kingdom. The only way to enter is to come, as the child came, at the call of Jesus Christ, and to take, as the child took, without a word, whatever place Jesus Christ may assign, whether in the centre, or on the far circumference of the circle of disciples, whether on the right or left hand of the King, or in the lowest rank of His servants.

Nor is this principle confined to the entrance. It is essential to all true Christian advancement. After one has entered the kingdom, it is expected of him that he shall continue childlike, tractable, unpretentious, and give no rein to that temper of self-aggrandisement which wants to push to the front and take the foremost place. "Whosoever therefore shall humble himself as this little child, the same is the greatest in the kingdom of heaven."

So the Saviour taught, and so He lived. He was the pattern of that humility which He inculcated. He exhibited no anxiety for station or fame among men, but simply devoted Himself to the work which the Father had given to Him to do.   Where the Father would place Him, there would He be.   What the Father would teach Him, that would He say.   Nothing was more repugnant to Him than the self-seeking temper which marked the Pharisees.   He would have His disciples breathe quite another spirit.   They should be willing to stand where He would place them, to go whither He might send them, to do what He might bid, to teach what He would command, happy as little children in trustfulness and docility.

2. A lesson from the child in His arms.

From St. Mark we learn that at this point of the conversation the Lord took up the little one in His arms, and so proceeded to teach His second lesson of humility, viz., the duty and privilege of receiving the lowly.   "Whosoever shall receive one of such little children in My name, receiveth Me ; and whosoever receiveth Me, receiveth not Me, but Him that sent Me."

The disciples, in disputing over their future rank, had been forgetting the mind and purpose of Christ, who had come to abase the proud and exalt the lowly. So He recalled them to the obligation and the blessedness of kindness to the weak, and a considerate reception of those whom an ambitious temper might push aside or treat with neglect. Such conduct to others, if actuated by a regard for His name, would be reckoned by Him as the most pleasing service they could render. If they would give themselves to the work of lowly love, receive and instruct little children or persons who were simple as babes in comparison with "the wise and prudent" of the time; if they would help the poor, teach the ignorant, mind not high things, but condescend to men of low estate, they would be rewarded in as well as for their service, for they would more fully receive Christ, and the Father in Christ, into their own hearts, and make an advance in the kingdom of heaven which could never be attained through the indulgence of a proud and self-exalting spirit.

What a stretch from the little child in Capernaum to the Father in heaven! But so it is: lowliness of spirit, with kind and patient love, is nearest to the Divine heart, and fraught with the loftiest blessing.

And what a lesson in theology ! Not through arduous speculations, or by the help of technical statements regarding God handed down from former times, do we reach and know Him, but by that harmony with Him which shows itself in receiving little ones, helping the weak, and manifesting to all the gentleness of Christ. Let us study in the house at Capernaum, for it is a great school of divinity. Let us look at Jesus there with the child in His arms, and learn how God thinks and feels—what God is. In Him are holiness, justice, and truth, but also sweetness, gentleness, love. He resists the proud, and gives grace to the lowly.

The Church visible has erred in seeking great things for herself, and coping with kingdoms of the world in titles, revenues, and dignities, while children have been neglected, mourners not comforted, and the poor have not had the gospel preached to them. Only when the Church is loving, patient, self-forgetful, absorbed in her Master's service and glory, can she be said to be the true exponent of the Father's will, and to approve herself as under the guidance of His Holy Spirit.

II. *Lessons of consolation.*

The Lord Jesus, receiving and caring for children and childlike disciples, is much displeased alike with any who endanger their consistency by putting a stumbling-block in their way to cause them to fall, and with any who despise those little ones as of small account, forgetting that they are precious in His sight.

In the Saviour's words, as reported by St. Matthew, there appear three guarantees for the safety of His "little ones :"—

1. The care of guardian angels (ver. 10). Men may deal hardly with the childlike followers of Jesus, but angels minister to them and encamp round about them ; and those are good angels who "behold the Father's face," *i.e.*, are in the Divine favour.

It does not follow from this that each individual has one guardian angel assigned to him as a good genius to watch over him from the cradle to the grave. Of this Scripture reveals nothing. Enough that to the good angels as heavenly servants is committed the care of the heirs of salvation.

There is joy in the presence of the angels over every one who is brought in a childlike spirit into the kingdom of God. Is this joy to be turned to weeping through the loss of such little ones after they have been found? And is the care of the angels to be defeated? Are those bright and loving spirits to watch in vain, and to be thwarted and disappointed after all? It cannot be. Therefore the little ones shall not perish.

2. The love of the Good Shepherd.* The Son of Man, the Lord of angels, has saved those little ones, and He will not suffer them to perish. There is no weakness in His purpose, no negligence in His oversight, no change in His love. He has given to them eternal life, and no one is able to pluck them out of His hand.

In regard to those who are actually children,

* The authenticity of Matt. xviii. 11 is uncertain, and the verse is omitted in the Revised Version ; but the thought remains in the short parable of verses 12, 13.

a fine passage occurs in the second part of the "Pilgrim's Progress." "By the river-side in the meadow there are cotes and folds for sheep, and a house built for the nourishing and bringing up of those lambs, the babes of those women that go on pilgrimage. Also there was here One that was intrusted with them, who could have compassion, and could gather the lambs with His arm, and carry them in His bosom. Now to the care of this Man Christiana admonished her four daughters to commit their little ones, that by those waters they might be housed, harboured, succoured, and nourished, and that none of them might be lacking in time to come. This Man, if any of them go astray, will bring them back again. He will also build up that which was broken, and will strengthen them that were sick. This Man will die before one of those committed to His trust shall be lost. So they were content to commit their little ones to Him." In a word, all young children who are committed to the Lord in faith, and all childlike Christians, are "safe in the arms of Jesus."

3. The will of the Father in heaven (ver.

14).   It is the Father's will which the Son interprets and fulfils in saving the lost.   It is the same supreme will which secures by the providence of the Son, the guidance of the Spirit, and the ministry of good angels, that none of the rescued ones shall perish.   It is the Father's good pleasure to give them the kingdom.   A stronger assurance, a more sublime guarantee, it is impossible to conceive.

"Not one of these little ones."   Not one! The Shepherd knows every sheep and lamb. The Father knows every child, and thinks of every one.   He has a smile for this child and correction for that; a promise for this one, and a warning for that, as each may require; but for every one He has love.   It is His will that of all the children who have trusted in Him, His Son Jesus shall lose none, but raise up every one at the last day.

XVIII.

THE EYE OF A NEEDLE.

"And Jesus said unto His disciples, Verily I say unto you, It is hard for a rich man to enter into the kingdom of heaven. And again I say unto you, It is easier for a camel to go through a needle's eye, than for a rich man to enter into the kingdom of God. And when the disciples heard it, they were astonished exceedingly, saying, Who then can be saved? And Jesus looking upon them said to them, With men this is impossible; but with God all things are possible."
—ST. MATT. xix. 23-26.

How naturally flowed the conversational teaching of Jesus Christ! Nothing was dragged in or forced. There was no formal and premeditated treatment of topics. The Master was content to take His theme from current incidents, employing upon them His unrivalled facility of extemporaneous illustration and suggestion.

Pharisees came to Him with a question about divorce, and He took occasion not only to lay down first principles on the sanctity of marriage, but to teach His disciples that it might be expedient for some of His servants to refrain from marriage, not for the base reason suggested by them, that marriage without facility for divorce would be an intolerable yoke, but for a much worthier cause, viz., that they might be more useful in the kingdom of heaven.

Then a rich young man accosted Him, strongly proclaiming his desire to keep any and every condition in order to perfection. The Master applied to him a hard test which he could not bear, and as the young man turned away with downcast countenance, this significant comment fell from the lips of Jesus, "It is hard for a rich man to enter into the kingdom of God."

This saying, like the former one about "eunuchs for the kingdom of heaven's sake," has been quoted to justify and exalt ascetic forms of Christian virtue. The states of celibacy or virginity and of voluntary poverty have been pronounced holy, and bound on men and women under vows of perpetual obligation. There is no ground for this in the sayings of our Lord. It even conflicts with common sense; for how can it be supposed that a religion which can find perfection only by methods which go to the destruction of society and of property has issued from an all-wise God? Voluntary celibacy and voluntary poverty may be the high duty of some men and women for special service to their Lord, but such sacrifices of natural rights are of an exceptional character, and should never be dictated as vows or regulations.

We can admire the self-denial of St. Paul, who, though he was under no vow of celibacy, and had the same right as St. Peter and other apostles to the married state, determined not to marry in order that he might be unhindered in his missionary journeys. We can admire the same resolution in modern missionaries who have followed his example; although for missionary work generally marriage is, on the whole, an advantage. But it is a very different thing to set forth celibacy as a "counsel of perfection," and enforce it on all who are recognised as official servants and handmaids of Christ in His Church. To do so is to misconstrue the teaching of our Lord, and to misconceive the best conditions of the Christian life.

In like manner we admire the self-denial of Joseph, surnamed Barnabas, who sold his land and devoted the money to the common purse of the persecuted Church at Jerusalem; and we rejoice to know that in such surrender of earthly goods for charity or for missionary service he has had a good many followers in ancient and modern times. But it would be wrong, and even absurd, to bid every Christian who would please the Lord strip himself of all worldly property.

It was from the story of the rich young man in the Gospel that the famous Anthony, the very patriarch of Monachism, inferred that it was his duty to abandon his ancestral estate and live in solitude and poverty. There is no question of the ardour and sincerity of the man; but as we read what history has to tell of the moral and social effects of Monachism, we cannot but reflect how much better it would have been for all Christendom if Anthony had lived on the estate which he inherited, and used his means and position for the honour of Christ and the gospel among the ignorant peasantry around, rather than have passed his life in the desert, injuring his own body by gratuitous hardships, maintaining mysterious combats with fiends, and so leading hundreds and thousands of misguided men into a similar pursuit of an illusive ascetic perfection.

Protestant Christianity has not been without noble instances of the renunciation of riches for Christ and the gospel. But even were the generous impulse more frequent than it is, it could seldom be carried into effect with a clear judgment and conscience, for a man of hereditary property is not free to give away what ought to pass to his descendants, and a man who has made his own fortune must recognise the reasonable claims or expectations of his family. Accordingly, the normal condition of things must be that the Church expects her people to give habitually a proportion of their income. Yet this, which should be easy for a rich man, is found to be difficult. As a rule, persons who have small or moderate incomes give away more in proportion than those do who enjoy affluence. Let our Lord's warning be remembered. It is hard for those who have riches to keep their hearts above them, and maintain in prosperity an entire devotedness to Christ and the gospel.

By such teaching the Saviour was secretly preparing His apostles for the days of trial which would come on them and on their brethren after His ascension, that they might be willing to have that common purse at Jerusalem, to which we have already adverted, and which put too great a strain on such half-hearted Christians as Ananias and Sapphira, and that afterwards they might "take joyfully the spoiling of their goods" rather than deny their Master's name. Already they had left all to follow Him. In that mind they must continue to the end, holding whatever might come into their possession in trust for higher ends than personal gratification—for the service of the Lord Jesus and the promotion of the kingdom of heaven.

Our Lord gave point to His teaching on this subject by an illustration—perhaps one in proverbial and popular use. He likened a rich man carrying great possessions, and trying with them to enter the heavenly kingdom, to a laden camel attempting to thread the eye of a needle. It has been suggested that the needle's eye was an expression in common use for a narrow gate into a city intended for foot-passengers only, and through which, if a camel could squeeze at all, it would first need to be unladen and entirely stripped of trappings and encumbrances. Very possibly this explanation may be right, but it is not necessary to scrutinise closely what is so obviously the language of hyperbole. The object is to stamp on the mind and memory the idea of extreme difficulty, and it has been shown by a great scholar * that a Talmudist used for the same purpose a phrase still more hyperbolical—" an elephant going through the eye of a needle."

Any one who has seen laden camels in the East will appreciate the illustration. It is quite impossible to pass them through a tight

* Dr. John Lightfoot's Harmony of the Four Evangelists, *in loc.*

place. If one comes to a passage too narrow or a gate too low, he simply stands and utters a cry. He must be unladen, and will forthwith lie down for the purpose. But he is a cumbrous creature at the best, and needs more room than any other quadruped that is known in Palestine.

The difficulty of the admission of rich men into the kingdom of heaven, emphasised by such a metaphor as this, greatly astonished the apostles. "They were exceedingly amazed, saying, 'Who then can be saved'?" The reason of this is that their thoughts still ran on a kingdom to be speedily restored to Israel, in which they should themselves hold high places and become both rich and powerful. Surely the adherence of men with great possessions should be welcomed, not discouraged. True that they were not greedy men, though one of them had "an itching palm." They followed Jesus for something better than wealth ; but if rich men were to be kept out of the kingdom, or admitted only on condition of reducing themselves to poverty, how could the cause of their Master prosper ? how could the kingdom come? Nay, with such restrictions, who could be saved? Those Galileans spoke with a perfectly ingenuous estimate of the importance of wealth—an estimate which, though it may not be so plainly avowed, prevails at this day all over the East. Everything is open to a rich man. Every religious privilege is conferred on him; every political advantage is secured by him. A poor man *may* be saved, but a rich man *must.*

Our Lord's way of thinking on this, as on all points, was original and unique. He neither sided with opulent and prosperous men, nor avoided them. He neither deferred to the rich to please them, nor inveighed against them to please the populace. His care was to show that a man's life consists not in an abundance of earthly possessions, and to give warning that the hold which such possessions take of the human heart vastly increases the difficulty of Christian discipleship. It may well be asked, Whence had this Man such calm wisdom above all the men of His time? How did He, who had grown up in a carpenter's house, and had no house of His own wherein to lay His head, come to possess this sublime superiority alike to the passion of covetousness and to the discontent of poverty?   He was a prophet, and more than a prophet.   He was the Son of God.

At the bewildered question of the apostles, Jesus looked on them with a significant expression, and uttered this memorable sentence —" With men this is impossible, but with God all things are possible."

This may be understood of salvation—the salvation of rich and poor alike.   So far as human merits and efforts reach, salvation is not merely difficult, but impossible.   No living man is able by any labours or endurances in his own strength, or within his own resources, to save himself from his sins or place himself within the kingdom of heaven. The thing is impossible.   But it is possible with God; it is work in which He delights, to save men by Christ Jesus.   He reconciles His enemies.   He recovers the lost.   He pardons the guilty.   He cleanses those whom sin has basely soiled.   He creates them anew in Christ Jesus. Salvation is a marvellous thing, but it is possible with God.

This, however, is not our conception of the Lord's meaning. We regard Him as having still in view the special difficulty of the salvation of the rich. The influence of great possessions on the heart had been shown in the recoil of the young man who had been sharply tested by the word of Jesus. His riches were more to him than all those aspirations after perfection which he had so ardently expressed. He wished to be good, nay, to be perfect ; but when the Master bade him part with his possessions and give all to the poor, He touched as with the point of a spear the weak point, or revealed as with a flash of light the secrets of the young man's heart. The inquirer thought that he loved God and his neighbour, but he did not do so with all his strength and mind. He loved riches more. So the meaning is this— with men it is impossible to leave all that one has in order to follow Jesus and have treasure in heaven. From natural generosity one may give away a great deal of money to charitable uses; and yet he clings to his possessions, and is careful not to impair them. Man trusts in riches if he has them; he craves them if he has them not. But with God even this is possible. His grace can make the poor contented and the rich self-denied. He knows how to teach and enable a Christian man to increase riches without craft or greed, to use riches as a steward for a Heavenly Master, or even to renounce riches if such sacrifice be necessary to a thorough obedience. He can keep one from trusting in uncertain riches, and lead him so to trust in the living God as to make the best of both worlds, following the Lord Jesus here with a free and honest heart, and here-after receiving recompense a hundredfold, with ample time to enjoy it; for he is an heir of eternal life.

XIX.

THE GNAT AND THE CAMEL.

"Woe unto you, Scribes and Pharisees, hypocrites! for ye tithe mint and anise and cummin, and have left undone the weightier matters of the law, judgment, and mercy, and faith: but these ye ought to have done, and not to have left the other undone. Ye blind guides, which strain out the gnat, and swallow the camel."—St. Matt. xxiii. 23, 24.

A most effective illustration this of a scrupulousness which is extreme and inconsistent—"Ye strain out the gnat, and swallow the camel." * We are supposed to look at one drinking water or wine from an open vessel. A gnat or small fly has got into the liquor—a thing that will occur in hot weather among ourselves, and that is sure to occur in the

---

* The appearance of "at" instead of "out" in the authorised version is due to a mere error of the press. The previous versions of Tyndale, Coverdale, and Cranmer have the correct rendering — "Strain out!" It is, at all events, a proof of the conservatism with which the text of the authorised version has been preserved, that even an obvious typographical error like this has never been amended.

East if a vessel containing any sweet liquor is left uncovered. He who would drink notices the small insect, and passes the sweetened water or wine through a fine cloth in order to strain it out. With gross inconsistency, however, he takes no notice of a far larger object, but gulps down the camel. The mention of this unwieldy creature is of course an instance of hyperbole, as in the other metaphor, already considered, of a camel going through the eye of a needle.

The Lord implied no censure on the pains taken to strain out the gnat. No person of nice habits could act otherwise. Indeed, a Jew had a special reason for being scrupulous in such a matter, for insects, as " flying swarming things," were unclean under his law. But then the camel was unclean also. The point of the reproof lay in the incongruity or inconsistency evinced by one who was extremely scrupulous in a small thing, and extremely unscrupulous in a great matter. Such was the charge which Christ brought against the Pharisees ; and it must be brought still against those who combine a very punctilious Christian profession with a lax or un-principled morality.

The language of Jesus Christ rose to the severity of invective against that pretentious sect which so constantly and so bitterly opposed His influence. No consideration for His own safety, or for the high esteem in which the Pharisees were popularly held, could induce Him to conceal or disguise His intense repugnance to those proud and selfish ceremonialists, whose consciences were so ostentatiously strict on small points and so shamefully lax on great matters.

It appears that the Pharisees were very punctilious about paying tithes of seeds which were grown in small quantities, and were of comparatively little value. Mint was grown for its pleasant odour; anise or dill and cummin for their aromatic flavour. These were cultivated, not for food, but for scents and relishes; and only a small quantity of each would be grown in a private garden for the use of a household. But the Pharisees all the more made a point of dedicating a tithe of these trifles, in order to sustain their high religious credit. A parallel case now would be for a Christian in good circumstances to present to the Church one-tenth of the value of the parsley, pepper, and mustard used in his household.

Now the Pharisees were observing the letter of the law, which said, " All the tithes of the land, whether of the seed of the land or of the fruit of the tree, is the Lord's; it is holy unto the Lord." *   And the Master recognised this when He said that these minute tithings should not be left undone. But the chief matters of obligation should be placed first. All very well to be obedient in the smallest details, but not at all well to put forward a pedantic attention to comparative trifles as an excuse or screen for neglecting serious duties. And such was the sin of the Pharisees. They did not disown, but in practice they omitted those " weightier matters of the law," which involved a far better test of devotion to the Lord than any amount of cheap punctilio.

The weightier matters of obligation were, and continue to be, these three :—(1.) Judg-

* Leviticus xxvii. 30.

ment, including equity in judging and rectitude in performing the duties of life. (2.) Mercy in unison with justice, as it is in God Himself. The Pharisees gave alms with a blowing of trumpets, but they did not love mercy. (3.) Faith or faithfulness, shown in honest dealing and in adherence to truth. The Pharisees knew that these were weighty matters of obligation, but found them irksome, and therefore omitted them, vainly thinking to compensate for the omission by extreme attention to the minutiæ of external obedience.

Our Lord's treatment of this grave error suggests two points for emphatic consideration in Christian doctrine and morals :—

I. *Inward qualities count for more than outward observances.*

The tendency to forget or reverse this principle has been very strong both in the House of Israel and in the Church of God. In the former, men would render sacrifice, but would not obey; would offer " the fat of rams " on the altar, but would not hearken to do the voice of Jehovah. Therefore were so many prophets sent to reform and correct the hollow ceremonialism of Israel. Samuel treated it with an almost scornful severity. Isaiah recognised that there was no stint in the supply of bullocks, lambs, and he-goats for the altar; much incense was used in the Temple; and the Sabbath and new-moon festivals were honoured with great show of piety; yet the Lord held the oblations to be vain, and the solemn assemblies a weariness, because the moral life was not bettered; the rulers and the people did not cease to do evil or learn to do well.

The barren externalism which had been the bane of the Jews' religion in earlier times showed itself in the days of Christ in an aggravated form in the Scribes and Pharisees, and stirred, as we have seen, the sacred indignation of Him who was the greatest of prophets. They relegated the ethics of religion to a subordinate place, and even omitted them. Jesus relegated the keeping of rites and customs and the punctilious attention to ceremonial details to the subordinate place, and set the great matters of God's law and of conformity to God's mind in the front of all.*

A tendency similar to that which was shown by the Pharisees has appeared under all forms of religion, and has been sharply satirised in both heathen and Christian literature. It is, however, most shameful in those who profess and call themselves Christians. Strange to read of those rough - handed Christians in the past who were unjust and rapacious, and yet imagined that by paying tithes, or taking sacraments, or endowing monasteries at death, they could secure the favour of God. But just as delusive the modern assumption that one may be false to his word, unkind in his family, unfair in his dealings, and yet by attention to Christian rites and ceremonies may find his way to heaven. One good reason, indeed, for resist-

---

* It is sometimes represented that Christ was indifferent to doctrine, and cared for the moral life only. This is not true to fact, nor is the opposition of doctrine to morals philosophically or historically just. Good doctrine and good morality are close friends and relations ; and they are best taught when taught together. The moral precepts of Jesus are not to be dissociated from His doctrine regarding God and salvation from sin.

ing the present-day craze for ceremonial in church is that the multiplication of forms is apt to feed the vain confidence of men in external homage, apart from the inward qualities of justice, mercy, and faith. We may not be able to extinguish the Pharisaic spirit, which, if it finds no food in one direction, will seek it in another, and is very hard to kill; but at all events we may cease from making that express provision for it which is involved in giving prominence to what is of mere external prescription in the appointments and vestures of religion, instead of laying the stress on inward purity and moral soundness.

II. *That a just sense of proportion is essential to a well-regulated Christian mind.*

It must be recognised that, even among things which are right, some are greater and some less. Some are to be done first and foremost, and come what will; others are to come behind, and not to be left undone. If the Pharisees had not lacked this sense of proportion, they could never have preferred the tithing of mint to justice, tithing of dill to mercy, and tithing of cummin to faith; nor would they have condemned the righteous and merciful Saviour because He led His disciples along a path through a cornfield or healed poor people on the Sabbath.

It is no infrequent thing to find a person who seems to be very religious curiously deficient in the sense of proportion. He cannot quite see what is great or what is small. If he be disposed to obstinacy and bigotry, he simply regards all that is plain to him as great; and all his tenets and regulations as equally great. If he be merely small-minded, by natural affinity he fastens keenly on small points. These are of the proper size for him; and he takes them to be quite large. Or if he be of a self-regarding mind, considering religion simply with reference to his own safety, he lays all the stress on the truths which are near himself, and has but a faint appreciation of those which are much more vast but more remote.

It marks the wisdom of Jesus Christ that He saw the just proportion of things, and, when He spoke of duty, distinguished the greater elements of godly obedience from the less. And as He taught so He lived, entering into no competition with the Pharisees regarding the minutiæ of ceremonial and tradition, but exhibiting a righteousness far exceeding that of the Scribes and Pharisees, a mercifulness with which their haughty temper had no sympathy, and a fidelity to God and to His own Divine mission from which no temptation could beguile or threat deter Him.

Away with the Pharisaic faults of ostentation and hypocrisy, and the false importance assigned to vexatious prescriptions and petty scruples! We require not so much to do this or that minute thing according to the letter of the law, as to have heart and will suffused with that spirit of devotion to the Lord which will carry us wisely through all details of conduct, and give breadth and consistency to all our new obedience. We want the Christ-like mind to survey the large scope of duty, and put the weightier matters first, while the lighter follow after.

XX.

WHITEWASHED TOMBS.

"Woe unto you, Scribes and Pharisees, hypocrites! for ye are like unto whited sepulchres, which outwardly appear beautiful, but inwardly are full of dead men's bones, and of all uncleanness. Even so ye also outwardly appear righteous unto men, but inwardly ye are full of hypocrisy and iniquity."—St. Matt. xxiii. 27, 28.

"Woe unto you! for ye are as the tombs which appear not, and the men that walk over them know it not."—St. Luke xi. 44.

GRAVES lie thick about Jerusalem. In the valley and on the hilly slopes about the modern city they everywhere meet the eye. They are not at all beautiful, nor are the cemeteries enclosed or kept with any care. Mohammedan tombs, as a rule, everywhere have a neglected appearance. If one is occasionally seen whitewashed, it is that of a recently departed friend or of a Moslem devotee; and if one should pass it on a Friday, he would probably see some persons praying or reciting verses of the Koran at the spot.

Jews have always buried their dead, without, however, lavishing on their tombs such signs of honour and affection as are increasingly conspicuous in Christian cemeteries. But it was an old custom with them to wash sepulchral stones once a year. A day was fixed for the purpose in the month Adar; and at the time when our Lord used this metaphor to characterise the Scribes and Pharisees, the tombs about Jerusalem had been recently whitewashed, and so were beautified for a season. As He spoke in the open air, the white stones must have been conspicuous on every side.

The object of this whitewashing, however, was not to embellish, but to point out the gravestone to the passer-by, that he might not tread on it or touch it. The law which pronounced unclean him who touched a dead body, or even a dead bone unwittingly, was extended by the later casuistry so as to count one ceremonially defiled who even stepped unintentionally over a grave or touched a tombstone. It is this which explains the saying of our Lord as reported by St. Luke. It amounts to a charge against the Pharisees of concealing their true character from the people, and spreading contamination while no one suspected them of evil. They were as graves which men walked over without knowing it. But the charge as reported by St. Matthew was apparently spoken at a later date, and gave the metaphor a different turn. The object of Jesus was to mark with emphatic censure the contrast between the outward religious profession of those hypocrites and their inward wickedness. For this end the illustration was most apposite. The Pharisees, like the newly-washed tombs around the city, were fair and white on the surface, but unclean and corrupt within.

. Jesus Christ wished to carry His hearers beyond the superficial conception of a defilement contracted by bodily touch and removed by "divers washings." He looked on the heart, and laid all the stress on the principles and motives which actuate the will and the conduct. It must be confessed that His followers have imperfectly learned the lesson, for there has been and is a great deal of hollow Christian profession. Not that there has been any doubt of the mind of Christ on the subject, or any question among Christians of the vileness of a conscious hypocrisy, but that men easily acquiesce in the failure to reach a high level of truth and virtue, and are content to pay their homage to the ideal by appearing to be what they really are not. Christianity as well as Judaism is infested by shams, and echoes to the sounding brass of vain talkers and canting rogues; but it is not to be held accountable for these as though they were its authorised representatives, any more than the law of Moses was to be blamed for the pretentious Scribes and Pharisees in the time of our Lord. Christianity, in so far as it learns of Christ, hates hypocrisy, and holds it vain to adorn or whitewash the outward profession so long as the inward man remains foul and dead in trespasses and sins.

Indeed, all forms and sorts of religion have brought to light the same tendency in men to make outward show do duty for inward reality; and all religious teachers of any note have tried to resist this, and have laboured to impress on their disciples the insufficiency of a merely prescriptive and ceremonial devotion. Thus Gaudama (Buddha) inveighed against the ostentatious devoteeism of the Brahmins in words which resemble expressions of our Lord. "What is the use of plaited hair, O fool? What of the raiment of goat-skins? Within thee there is ravening, but the outside thou makest clean." * How like the language of Christ about false prophets attired in sheep-skins, who inwardly were ravening wolves! As it is now seen, Buddhism has sunk deplorably from its founder's platform. It has multiplied ceremonial and superstitious usages, and crushed its original spiritual philosophy under a mass of ignorant and tedious formalism. In fact, its degeneracy has in no small degree resembled the corruption of Christianity from its primitive spiritual simplicity. But its founder was no dull formalist. We do not place Gaudama on any pedestal of comparison with Jesus Christ, but it is only fair to him to

* Titcomb's Short Chapters on Buddhism, p. 167.

remember that he emphatically put purity and virtue above all shows and observances of piety.   He charged his followers to put away impure thoughts, and not deem it enough to observe external rules or render temple offerings.

Every reader of the Old Testament knows how earnestly the prophets of Judah and Israel protested against the offering of a formal worship and seeming obedience to 'Jehovah, while His laws were broken, and the hearts of princes, priests, and people alike went after the gods and vices of the heathen. Jesus Christ on this subject simply followed the prophets of His nation ; but He brought to this theme a keener insight into human nature, and that more intense abhorrence of unreality which belonged to Him as the Witness for God absolutely faithful and true.

By the example of the Lord Jesus, and by the very nature of the kingdom of God, public teachers of Christianity are bound to go straight to the central question of inward purification and inward spiritual life.   It is not at all enough to inveigh against wilful hypocrisy, or

against a thin veneer of religion pretending to
be a solid substance. Such invective is easy
and popular, but it may be overdone or mis-
directed. After all, there is not nearly so much
dissimulation in Churches as there is unworthy
contentment with the form of godliness without the power. And if this be prevalent, how
unwise and mischievous is the increase of ceremonial in church service! Reverent forms of
worship there ought to be, but the multiplication of formalities and the emphasis laid on
ritual and on consecrated places and vessels
lead men in the wrong direction, and encourage
that regard to outward show which it is so
necessary to discourage and reduce. Ritual-
ism no doubt means well. It would employ
that which is without in order to influence
that which is within. But the way of Christ
is the reverse of this. It is to cleanse a man
inwardly through the belief of the truth, and
so to influence his worship and his daily walk.

Those who have gone most deeply into the
problem of the improvement of society and
the elevation of the more depressed and degraded classes, have been compelled to see

that a beginning must be made at the very springs of inward life and character. Repression of facilities for evil indulgence is of some use, and the providing of helps and advantages for the formation of decent and virtuous habits may be of very considerable service ; but there is no effective drying up of social vices or victory over squalid conditions and base indulgences till new convictions, motives, and sentiments are brought into the breasts of men. Therefore it takes a high-souled man to be a true reformer.   There is no better actual to be reached without a finer and loftier ideal.

> " Subsist no rules of life outside of life,
> No perfect manners without Christian souls ;
> The Christ Himself had been no lawgiver
> Unless He had given the life too with the law." *

The higher we rise in our aims and the more we deal with the moral and spiritual life, the more do we find that everything depends on inward faith and feeling. The forms and apparatus of religion may be provided and maintained with diligence, and even with profusion ; and it may appear as though religion

* Aurora Leigh.

were greatly flourishing, and the kingdom of heaven were at hand. Yet the show may be quite fallacious and misleading. Religion may be faint and low. Vain and self-righteous men greatly affect outward shows of piety. Ignorant and superstitious men put their trust in ritual. Even wicked men may take to church-going for a pretence. Nothing is really gained till we are inwardly cleansed and renewed, so that fresh convictions of truth and duty occupy the soul, and new beliefs, hopes, and loves elevate the character and direct the life.

Why did not Jesus Christ, if He was the Son of God, reconstruct the world? Why did He not with a flash of Divine power put down the horrible evils and tyrannies under which the nations groaned, and set up the city of God and the reign of righteousness? It is easy to put such questions. We do not attempt a complete answer. We are content to point out that a slow process of working is more Divine than a rapid one; and in this instance we may perhaps render a reason why it is so. The evil which was in the world when Jesus Christ dwelt among men was rooted not in circumstances, or even in institutions—though these last were tainted by it and tended in turn to increase it—but in the heart of man; and therefore the remedy which the Divine Redeemer and Healer saw fit to apply was not a subversion of institutions, or a hasty alteration of the social environment which men had made for themselves, but a new birth of the individual, involving a new growth of moral sentiment and life, which has only to increase and multiply in order to spread a blessed change through families, tribes, and nations, reform institutions, reconstruct society, and renew the face of the world.

Great thinkers, great dreamers have imagined a new republic or a peaceful kingdom, moulding its people to wisdom and virtue by wise statutes and customs. Our religion has such a kingdom in sure promise, but proposes to reach it in a manner that seems slow and yet is very certain. This man and that man are born again. This house and that house are brought under the hallowing power of one or more spiritual persons dwell-

ing there.   Outward professions are good only
in so far as they express inward life.   But
wherever there is heaven-born life there is
harmony with God; and the increase of such
harmony is the setting up of the kingdom of
heaven.

Nothing is gained by whitewash or varnish.
God is not mocked, and even man is not
long imposed on by a vain show of devotion.
We once heard Father Taylor, a noted preacher
to sailors in America, pray that men who
thought themselves good and were not might
be undeceived; and he cried, "Lord, take off
the whitewash!"

XXI.

"THAT FOX."

"In that very hour there came certain Pharisees, saying to Him, Get thee out, and go hence ; for Herod would fain kill Thee. And He said unto them, Go and say to that fox, Behold, I cast out devils and perform cures to-day and to-morrow, and the third day I am perfected."—St. Luke xiii. 31, 32.

THE attempt of the Pharisees to frighten Jesus Christ out of Perea drew from Him a prompt and sharp rejoinder. Their statement that Herod meant to kill Him may have been a pure invention on their part, for we are told afterwards that Herod had long been desirous to see Jesus ; and when he did see Him as a prisoner at Jerusalem, his bearing towards our Lord was one of heartless levity rather than of truculence or malice.* Yet it may be that the Tetrarch wished to hasten the departure of the Galilean Prophet from the region beyond Jordan, and therefore caused a report to go out

* St. Luke xxiii. 8-11.

that he meant to do to Jesus as he had done to John the Baptist. If so, he may have instigated those Pharisees to carry the report to our Saviour, and to urge Him to save Himself by at once escaping out of Herod's province into that which was governed by Pontius Pilate. Something of the sort seems to us probable from the circumstance that our Lord not merely gave an answer to the Pharisees, which would have been enough if their word of alarm had been a mere audacious lie devised by themselves, but charged them to take back His reply to Herod—" that fox," that creature of cunning and deceit.

The answer was to the effect that no such threats could influence the purpose or in the least degree accelerate the movements of the Nazarene. His work was near an end, but He would have no hurry or panic. He would cast out demons and perform cures to the last day that His predestined stay in Perea would permit. If Herod wished to put a hasty stop to such works, so much to the discredit of Herod. As for the menace to His life, Jesus despised it. He was going up to Jerusalem, knowing that He would be killed. But Herod could not kill Him. At the outset of His ministry an angry crowd in Galilee had tried to make an end of Him, but they could not.[*] The Prophet could not die but at Jerusalem.

The metaphor here was in the opprobrious epithet applied to Herod Antipas—"that fox." Evidently it expressed, and was meant to express, that the Lord Jesus saw through and despised the cunning wiles of the Tetrarch. Many writers on the Gospels, both in Germany and among ourselves, have been anxious to protect our Saviour from the charge of speaking disrespectfully of a ruler, and have therefore tried to show that this epithet was in reality hurled against the Pharisees, who had affected so much solicitude for His life. Now we know that Jesus Christ did not spare epithets when He condemned the Pharisees; but He spoke them directly, not indirectly or by implication. He called them hypocrites and blind, and compared them, as we have seen, to whitewashed tombs. In the present case, it is as plain as words

[*] Chap. iv. 28–30.

can make it that Jesus stigmatised Herod as "that fox." The man was a selfish intriguer, neither good nor strong, but cunning, subservient to those above him, a sort of jackal to the imperial lion at Rome, but ruthless to any who were beneath him and within his grasp. "If ever there was a man who richly deserved contempt, it was the paltry, perjured princeling—false to his religion, false to his nation, false to his friends, false to his brethren, false to his wife—to whom Jesus gave the name of ' that fox.'" *

Probably it was this metaphor that suggested to Jesus that of the hen protecting her brood, which immediately follows. He looked on Herod and men of his stamp as devourers of the people. As for Himself, He might seem to be weak and unable to save Himself, but He was the best friend of the people; and if they would only gather to Him, He would cover them with the wings of His protection, so that no fox could do them hurt. But the Pharisees, and ultimately the misguided people too, took part with the fox against Him.

* Farrar : Life of Christ, vol. ii. p. 98, 11th ed.

The epithet certainly startles one. It must have sounded to the Pharisees like the crack of a whip. But there is no need to apologise for it as though it were unworthy of Him who was meek and lowly in heart, and had fallen from His lips incautiously. It was calmly spoken, and proceeded from a just feeling of scorn for a tricky and crafty character. And why should it be thought strange that Jesus could entertain and express a feeling of scorn for what is mean and wicked? He spoke forth His scorn, and even His indignation, at other times; why not also His contempt for the despicable ruler who had beheaded John the Baptist for a whim, and now, as the Pharisees reported, would fain kill One who was doing nothing but good to his subjects, casting out demons and performing cures?

Some of our moralists assert too roundly that mortal man has no right to feel contempt. There is a contempt that is ignoble, and there is a contempt that is noble. The ignoble is that which rests on mere conventionalism and prejudice, as when one despises another for being less highly born or less richly provided than himself. It flourishes among conventional professors of religion who yet sing the praises of humility. It was a marked characteristic of the Pharisees, who " trusted in themselves that they were righteous, and despised others." Such hauteur could not find place in the breast of our Saviour, and ought not to be harboured by any Christian. Wherever it enters it hardens the heart, dries up the sympathies, inflates the sense of self-importance, and induces a cold indifference to the wants and woes of others. But there is a noble scorn that may dwell in the heart along with tender compassion and fervent love. If there be a genuine appreciation of what is good and true, the obverse side of it must be a healthy contempt for what is wicked and false. When an honest man hears a boaster or a liar speak, or notices a mean and foxy fellow at his tricks, what can he feel but scorn? Why should he not feel it? And when a man detects himself in some cheating phrase or subtle manœuvre to outwit the simple, can he do better than despise himself?

In the mouth and in the heart of Jesus Christ there was no guile, and we may rest assured that those who please Him are the men of a simple faith, candid speech, and honest purpose. That man cannot be His disciple who breathes intrigue and practises deceit, and so is liable to be described by the Lord's withering epithet—" that fox."

XXII.

THE HEN AND CHICKENS.

"O Jerusalem, Jerusalem, which killeth the prophets, and stoneth them that are sent unto her! how often would I have gathered thy children together, even as a hen gathereth her chickens under her wings, and ye would not!"—ST. MATT. xxiii. 37.

"O Jerusalem, Jerusalem, which killeth the prophets, and stoneth them that are sent unto her! how often would I have gathered thy children together, even as a hen gathereth her own brood under her wings, and ye would not!"—ST. LUKE xiii. 34.

THE English translation, following the Vulgate, makes the illustration even more homely than need be. Our Lord said, "As a bird gathers her young under her wings." The translators fix on a particular bird — the poultry hen. Let it be so. No bird can better illustrate our Lord's meaning, and His word carries such intrinsic dignity that it does not need to fear the familiarity of a metaphor.

The object was to indicate the Saviour's

feeling for the people of Jerusalem in view of their city's hastening doom. If He had added nothing to the parable of the vineyard and the husbandman, and the terrible statement which followed it regarding the utter destruction of those who were to reject "the chief corner-stone," * it might have been inferred that His only feeling was one of stern displeasure ; but the saying now before us, coming after those warnings, revealed a mos. pathetic sorrow—the same which afterwards showed itself in tears and reproaches as He beheld the city on the way from Bethany. This was indeed returning love for hatred, since Jerusalem was the headquarters of the opposition which He encountered ; the rulers were bitter against Him ; and the general population had never shown to Him even as much respect as did the inhabitants of the northern towns and villages. But He looked on it as the seat of His father David's throne, and of the Temple, His Heavenly Father's house. There centred the national life and hope of the people who were by Messianic

* St. Matt. xxi. 33-44.

right especially His own. And this sorrowful apostrophe broke from Him as He thought of this city refusing and maltreating so many prophets—a wickedness about to come to the full in the rejection and crucifixion of Himself.

When Jehovah brought Israel out of Egypt, He bore them as " on eagle's wings." * Such was the Old Testament metaphor for strength. The eagle will bear her young on her own wide pinions to their rocky nest; and so the Lord bore and carried the tribes to the rocks of Sinai and Horeb. But now the question was of protecting the people of Jerusalem from impending judgment, and the simile to be used must suggest tenderness and sure defence. So the Lord illustrated His willingness to save by the covering wings of a motherbird extended over her brood.

The maternal love and courage of birds have been celebrated in the literature of all nations. Even the Mussulman admires it; witness the Moslem story of the white dove. One came before Mohammed with two fledglings tied up in a cloth, which he had taken from the

* Exodus xix. 4.

wood.   The mother dove had bravely followed. Mohammed commanded that the cloth should be opened; on which the dove flew down, and covered her trembling offspring with her wings.   Then the Prophet directed that the mother and her young should be restored unhurt to the nest in the wood, and took the opportunity to teach a good lesson :—

> " From Allah's self cometh this wondrous love ;
> Yea, and I swear by Him who sent me here,
> He is more tender than a nursing dove,
> More pitiful to men than she to these." *

To appreciate the feeling of Jesus Christ for Jerusalem, we must remember how complete was His knowledge of its sin.   He called to mind all its blood-guiltiness in connection with prophets and faithful witnesses for God. He foresaw that it would soon cut off His own life, that of His martyr Stephen, that of His apostle James, would have His apostle Peter in prison, and would try to destroy His apostle Paul.   Yet He lamented over that great city, and His compassion yearned to rescue its people from destruction.

* Edwin Arnold's Pearls of the Faith, p. 275.

" How often would I have gathered you!"
Most of the commentators understand this
of the Lord's feeling for Jerusalem before He
came in the flesh as well as after. They
suppose that as, in thinking of Jerusalem's
sin, He surveyed the past ages of resistance
to the voices of the prophets, as also in
describing the Divine willingness to save
Jerusalem and the Jews, He looked all down
the past ages of prophetic calls of repentance
and messages of grace. It may be so. Who
can determine the limits of our Saviour's
thought? But as a matter of exact interpretation, we hold that Jesus referred to the
opportunities which He had given to Jerusalem in His personal ministry. He carefully
distinguished His own ministry from that of
preceding prophets in the parable of the
vineyard, and had not even represented Himself as having sent those prophets. It was
the Father who had sent the prophets, and
finally sent Him. He referred, therefore, as
it seems to us, to the repeated visits which
He had paid to Jerusalem at personal risk,
and His willingness on each occasion to

receive the people of that guilty city under the wings of His protection. But they had never flocked to Him ; they would not.

Let it not be thought strange that the will of the people of Jerusalem should be allowed to resist and defeat the mercy of the Son of God. The whole history of the nation was one of often-repeated resistance to the will of Jehovah, and rejection of His grace. The Lord desired to save, but never would force salvation on any nation or on any creature. Indeed, a forced salvation would be futile, and mercy received against one's will could do no good. So the Jews were made welcome to come to Jesus Christ that they might have life, but, if they would not come, they must take the consequences. We are glad to know that thousands in Jerusalem afterwards turned to the Lord Jesus when He was preached to them in the power of the Spirit, but the mass of the population did not because they would not, and would not because they were blinded by a sort of self-righteous fanaticism. To this day the relations subsisting between Jesus Christ and the Jewish nation at large throughout the world may be expressed in His own words, " I would, but ye would not." *

The illustration used by our Lord implied that danger was at hand. Observe a hen in the open field, happy with her chickens running about her, picking and chirping in the sunshine. Suddenly a hawk appears in the air, or some mischievous animal comes slyly over the ground. On the instant the hen calls her brood to her, covers them with her wings, and is ready for their defence. Timid enough at other times, she is brave for her chickens, and will die rather than let one of them be lost. So the Lord Jesus, perceiving the danger which hovered over Jerusalem long before the Jews were aware of it, was willing to cover and save them. So also is it in every age and

---

* " Professor Delitzsch's Hebrew New Testament is much appreciated by the Jews of Baghdad. . . . In the desert, where we are at present encamped in tents, on the highway to Babylon, I am now sitting with five, who possibly may be direct descendants of those who refused to return to their own land. Had Professor Delitzsch seen the tears that rolled down from their eyes on my reading to them from his translation our Saviour's touching words in Matt. xxiii. 37–39, I am sure he would feel a thousand times compensated for his labours." —*Report of British and Foreign Bible Society for* 1884. p. 191.

every nation.   He who is the Saviour of the world sees the approaching perdition of ungodly men, and is willing to deliver them. Those who come to Him He will in no wise cast out.

The illustration of the hen and chickens was sure to catch the imagination of John Bunyan, and he has worked it out with characteristic ingenuity in the second part of the " Pilgrim's Progress."   The Interpreter led Christiana, Mercy, and the children " into a room where was a hen with chickens, and bade them observe a while. . . . So they gave heed, and perceived a fourfold method of the hen towards her chickens. (1.) She had a common call, and that she hath all the day long. (2.) She had a special call, and that she had but sometimes. (3.) She had a brooding note. (4.) She had an outcry. Now, said he, compare this bird to your King, and those chickens to His obedient ones. He has a common call and a special call. He has also a brooding voice for those that are under His wing; and He has an outcry, to give the alarm when He seeth the enemy coming."

It belongs to the theological school of which Bunyan was a staunch adherent to mark a distinction between the common call to salvation and the special or effectual call, the former being the invitation of the gospel, the latter that invitation as enforced and made to take effect by the power of the Holy Ghost. But enough for the elucidation · of our present topic that Christ is willing to gather sinners and save them—an assurance which is call sufficient to warrant all who hear it to come to Him, and to condemn all those who hear it and refuse compliance.

What a simple way of salvation! And how sure and perfect the defence! When lambs are startled, they run to the ewes; the kids to the she-goats. Among the fiercest animals, the young run to their mothers for protection, and these will guard their offspring at whatever peril to themselves. But no quadruped, wild or tame, can cover her young so completely as a bird can do with her folding wings. Therefore is this last the apt illustration of the sufficiency of Christ to save. Those who trust in Him are completely covered by His righteousness and strength.

On this wise has Divine salvation always been revealed. The Psalms frequently refer to the favour and protection of Jehovah as the shadow of outstretched wings.* So the ancients made the Most High their refuge, and so are all Christians saved and kept in the state of salvation simply by coming to the Lord Jesus and abiding in Him.

Our Redeemer's lament over Jerusalem shows what His heart is toward all mankind. It is a grief to Him to have His offer of salvation slighted, a joy to have it embraced. How unhappy the mother-bird while any of her brood continue astray and heedless of her call! How glad when she knows that they are all with her, trusting to her love and care! Her joy is greater than theirs, because she understands better than they do both their danger and their weakness. So Jesus Christ, who grieved so deeply over Jerusalem and her children, has His Spirit vexed when men who have been

* Ps. xvii. 8 ; xxxvi. 7 ; lvii. 1 ; lxi. 4 ; lxiii. 7 ; xci. 4.

called by His gospel turn away. He rejoices over every one who obeys the gospel more than the saved sinner can rejoice, for no one knows as He knows the awfulness of that perdition from which He rescues His people, or their weakness and hopelessness before the impending judgment.

What manner of persons Christians ought to be! What joy of faith, what restfulness of love should be under the covert of His wings! What nearness, too, to one another, and what obligation to brotherly kindness! The brood are packed very closely under the hen. Whatever little disputes and rivalries they may have had as they ran about the farmyard, the chickens must not quarrel in their hiding-place under the wing. There they dwell together in unity ; and the hen, by her love to them and her "brooding note," teaches them to love one another. Surely those who are in Christ must also learn to make room for one another, forbear one another in love, and keep one another warm in fellowship.

The "day approaching" is that of the glory

of Christ, and of our "gathering together to Him." In that day all His saints will be grouped around Him; but it will be too late for sinners who rejected His gospel to cry— "Make room for me also! Saviour, take me in!" The day for the gathering in grace is now, and it is fleeting fast away.

> "'To-day the Saviour calls !
> For refuge fly ;
> The storm of vengeance falls,
> Ruin is nigh.'"

"He shall cover thee with His feathers, and under His wings shalt thou trust."

XXIII.

LIGHTNING.

" For as the lightning cometh forth from the east, and is seen even unto the west; so shall be the coming of the Son of Man."—St. Matt. xxiv. 27.

A FLASH of lightning is proverbial as an illustration of suddenness and swiftness. Our greatest poet writes of the—

> " Momentary and sight-outrunning lightnings,
> Precursors of the dreadful thunder-claps." *

But the point of comparison intended by our Lord's use of this metaphor is not so much the suddenness of the flash, as the wide visibility of lightning. No matter in what direction you are looking, you see it. It comes out of the East, and shines even to the West, *i.e.*, it seems to light up with its vivid sheen all the acrial space within our

* The Tempest, act i. scene 2.

horizon.   The phrase is used in a popular sense, and does not assume to set forth the movement of lightning with scientific precision.   It is an allusion to what all have observed in thunderstorms; a sudden vivid light catches every eye when—

"From cloud to cloud the rending lightnings rage." *

And this is taken by Christ as an illustration of His own universal visibility at the era of His second and glorious appearing. He will come in the clouds of heaven, and every eye shall see Him.   "All the tribes of the earth shall mourn, and shall see the Son of Man coming on the clouds of heaven with power and great glory." †

I. This is stated to put the disciples on their guard against pseudo - Christs.   Such persons were to arise in the later and much-troubled years of the Jewish state.   Though fanatics and impostors, they were to gather adherents in that time of confusion and desperation.

* Thomson.   † Ver. 30.

It is matter of history that such men did appear, and deluded many into an acceptance of their claims by a pretence of wonder-working, and by promising to the Jews miraculous help from heaven to raise the siege of Jerusalem and drive away the Roman armies. It is to be feared that similar deceivers will play a baleful part in Christendom before a greater judgment falls. There will be false Christs and false prophets in the last days; but such persons will avoid close scrutiny of their character and claims. "It is at once the impostor's policy and the fanatic's instinct to deny facilities for full and impartial examination. Hence the pretended Christ will probably either betake himself to the desert or screen himself in some chamber where there will be comparative difficulty of access and of sifting investigation." * Quite different was the method of the true Christ, who bore Himself towards all classes of the people with the utmost candour and simplicity. Thus He was able to say to the high priest, "I have

* Morrison's Comm. *in loc.*

spoken openly to the world; I ever taught in synagogues and in the temple, where all the Jews come together; and in secret spake I nothing." * So it was at His first coming, and at the second the visibility will be on a greater and more splendid scale. There will be no haze of uncertainty or half concealment, but, " as the lightning cometh forth from the east, and is seen even unto the west, so shall be the coming of the Son of Man."

II. This is fatal to a modern theory of a secret coming of the Lord in the air, and a secret rapture of some of the saints to meet Him. It is put forth by certain confident students of prophecy that the Lord is to come to some point or halting-place in the aerial firmament unperceived by the tribes and nations of the earth; and that such saints as are prepared and watchful will in a secret manner be caught up to join Him and dwell with Him in mid-air, reigning from thence over the earth, and after a time re-descending with Him to the earth in His glorious train.

* St. John xviii. 20.

Now of the rapture of the saints to "meet the Lord in the air" there is no room to doubt; but the notion of a secret coming, responded to by a secret rapture, and of a halting-place for months or years in the air that surrounds our globe, is, so far as we understand the Scriptures, not only without their sanction, but contrary to their teaching.

It is against Scripture to suppose that only some of the living saints will "be caught up." St. Paul says, "We who are alive and remain," in distinction from "the dead in Christ." [*] First, those who have fallen asleep will be raised; then those who have not slept will be changed. So shall the whole Church of the saints be stirred up to meet the King of Glory.

Also the theory of a long arrest of the Lord's descent, and of a halt in mid-air for a considerable period, is, to say the least, unsupported by the Bible, and can scarcely be thought of with seriousness. To say that the saints go up to meet the Lord, as the wise virgins in the parable went forth to meet the bridegroom, is

* 1 Thess. iv. 17.

one thing; to say that He will stay at the point at which they meet Him, and, suspending His progress, dwell with them in a kind of aerial city, is another thing altogether, and one for which we find no ground in prophecy.

But the strongest objection of all is to the notion of a coming of Jesus Christ which, at least up to a certain point and for a certain period, will be unnoticed by the nations of the earth, bringing no terror to the ungodly, and not even known by the majority of professed Christians. This seems to us to be directly at variance with the words of Christ and His apostles. When the flash of lightning across the open sky is kept secret from the eyes of men, then, and not till then, can we believe in a secret advent of the Lord; and when the thunder which follows the flash can be heard by some men only, and not by others who stand around them, then, and not till then, can we believe in mysterious silence covering an event which is to be announced by "the voice of the archangel and the trump of God."

In fact, this is one of the plainest things revealed to us about the second advent, that it will be bright with heavenly glory and universally conspicuous. There are other accompaniments and results of that sublime event which, though they be indicated on the prophetic page, it is difficult, perhaps impossible, for us, with our present knowledge, to arrange in the order in which they will appear. It may be well to set down here some thoughts on the subject.

The disciples, sitting with their Master on the Mount of Olives, put to Him three questions in a breath as to (1) the date of the overthrow of the Temple; (2) that of His own second coming; and (3) that of the end of the world, or consummation of the age.* They assumed that these events would be synchronous, or nearly so. Accordingly, in the reply of Christ, as reported by the Evangelist, no notice is taken of the long space of time which, as we know, intervenes between the fall of Jerusalem and its Temple and the consummation of the age, as we understand the term ; but the Lord

* Ver. 3.

indicated that for both of those catastrophes He would come.

All through sacred prophecy we find examples of this method. There is an apparently simultaneous prevision of nearer events and of those greater ultimate issues which the nearer illustrate and forecast. Two or more future blessings or judgments are taken together, because the less prepares for the greater, or the proximate suggests and guarantees the remote. And as when one has in perspective the crests of a mountain range, he has no vision of the gaps and valleys between, so the prophetic eye takes no note of intervals, leaps over centuries, and glances quickly from one future event to another, provided that they lie in the same range and at the same angle of vision. So the prophetic language grasps the near and the distant together, and sometimes applies to the near and the smaller event expressions which in their fulness are appropriate only to the farther and the greater. Thus in the Psalter it is not easy to separate the language which was descriptive of the prosperous kingdom of David and Solomon from that which

is satisfied only in the kingdom of Christ;
and in the books of the prophets, oracles
regarding the restoration of the Jews from
their captivity in Babylon are twined together
with predictions of a return from a much
longer and further dispersion, and of favour to
be restored to Israel in the latter days. After
the same manner, in this discourse on the
Mount of Olives, Jesus Christ brought together a nearer and a farther horizon of judgment, each of them involving His own coming
with mighty power.

For the destruction of Jerusalem and the
Temple, as of old time for the arrest of the
building of Babel, the Lord's coming down
was potential, not personal and visible. The
second coming proper is yet to be, and it will
be visible as lightning, and personal, because
the first coming was so and the ascension was
so, and the angels said to the men of Galilee,
" This Jesus, who has been received up from
you into heaven, shall so come in like manner
as ye have beheld Him going to heaven." *

The results of the Lord's coming are vari-

* Acts i. 11.

ously set forth in New Testament prophecy, but the statements may be grouped under these three heads.   He comes—

1. To receive the Bride, the Church, into His glory.

2. To receive the kingdom, and reign with His saints.

3. To judge the world in righteousness.

How far these objects may be simultaneous, or whether they follow each other, and if so, in what order and at what intervals of time, it is hard to tell, and impossible to decide with certainty.   It should be remembered that what is a day with the Lord may be a thousand years, and the day of His coming, though introduced suddenly, may stretch out into a long age.   Then some of the events foretold of that day may occur in the morning, some at noon, and some in the evening, *i.e.*, some at the dawn, some in the middle, and others at the close of a long period of our Lord's epiphany in power and great glory.

One thing is very sure, if we have rightly understood the metaphor of the lightning. To mockers, walking after their own lusts, and

asking, " Where is the promise of His coming ?" the advent of our Lord will bring a
dreadful surprise ; and self-complacent persons who assure themselves of peace and
safety shall find that sudden destruction has
come upon them. How many that laugh now
shall then mourn and weep!

XXIV.

VULTURES.

"Wheresoever the carcase is, there will the eagles be gathered together."—ST. MATT. xxiv. 28.

"And they answering say unto him, Where, Lord? And he said unto them, Where the body is, thither will the eagles also be gathered together."—ST. LUKE xvii. 37.

THE Revised Version retains "eagles" in the text, but puts "vultures" in the margin. There can be no doubt that the reference is to those yellow vultures and carrion kites which abound in such regions as Palestine, and serve a good purpose in clearing away putrid carcases. Dogs are the scavengers of the towns, vultures, kites, and ravens of the country; and these have not to wait the orders of sanitary inspectors, but of themselves promptly and unerringly find their proper prey, and remove offensive matter with a thoroughness which no human arrangements could ensure.

Mention of such creatures may not please a fastidious taste; but our Lord saw it needful to speak of judgment as well as of mercy, and of the sweeping away of what is morally offensive as well as of the encouragement of all that is morally sweet and beautiful. For this end He chose the metaphor that best suited His theme. He referred His hearers to that which they must have often seen —the gathering of birds of prey from all quarters to fasten on a carcase lying exposed on some hillside or in some valley of Judea or Galilee.

The same figure is employed by two of the ancient prophets,* and in the Book of Revelation.† And all the passages in which it occurs have reference to an era of coming judgment and a stern victory over the enemies of the Lord. Not giving due consideration to the parallel passages, many interpreters have gone wonderfully astray in regard to our Saviour's meaning in the use of this metaphor.

* Hab. i. 8; Ezek. xxxix. 17-20.　　† Rev. xix. 17, 18.

They have supposed that the body referred to
is that of Christ Himself, slain for us, and
that "the eagles" denote the believers who
gather together and feed on the holy sacrifice.
It is astonishing to find even Calvin, that
most judicious commentator, adopting an interpretation so unnatural, and so painful to
every feeling of reverence.*

The true meaning is not hard to be found
if we keep in view two guiding considerations:
(1.) That this saying occurs in a prophecy
of tribulation and judgment; and (2.) That
the vulture is emphatically a bird of prey,
and suggests havoc and death.

We find in our Lord's reference to the
vultures—

I. *A strong hint or presage of the fall of
Jerusalem before the Romans.*

This was the primary, though by no means
the only, subject treated of in the Lord's discourse.

* The good sense of Calvin, however, revolted at the suggestion of previous commentators, that the odour of the
decaying carcase attracting the foul birds represented the
attraction which the death of Christ has for the elect. He

Before the tribes entered the land of promise, Moses warned them that if they should prove disobedient to Jehovah He would bring against them a nation from far "as an eagle flieth." * The prophet Habakkuk foresaw the fulfilment of this menace in the invasion of the land and capture of Jerusalem by armies from Babylon; and, as we have seen, he used the same figure to describe what he foresaw. It was as though vultures fastened on the spiritless God-forsaken city and laid it waste. But in the days of the gospel a greater and more terrible woe was drawing nigh. The Lord Jesus saw it with clear though saddened eyes, and warned His disciples that the city which was about to reject and crucify Him would wax worse and worse, and become a mere carcase for vultures from afar. Its Temple would be desolate; its citizens would be torn by the spirit of faction and hatred. What had been reckoned a holy city would

gave the idea another turn, and made the best of it thus :—
" Si tanta est in avibus sagacitas, ut ex remotis locis ad cadaver unum multæ conveniant, turpe esse fidelibus, non aggregari ad vitæ Auctorem, quo solo vere pascuntur."

* Deut. xxviii. 49.

become a mere quarry for birds of prey. Lo! the Roman armies, bearing eagles on their standards, hastening from afar, and swooping down on that wicked and infatuated Jerusalem. The Hebrew Christians, who had spiritual life in them, were forewarned by the Saviour's words, and escaped from the city before it was closely invested. Without them Jerusalem was dead and corrupt; so the Roman eagles got the carcase.

II. *An indication of wider and sorer judgments at the last day.*

Prior to the second coming of Christ is to be a period of tribulation and of abounding iniquity. We gather from the Book of Revelation * that the nations will be misled by the Beast and the False Prophet, *i.e.*, by unhallowed strength and unhallowed wisdom, and make war against Him who sits on the heavenly throne. Then shall those nations be judged and overthrown by the King of Kings and Lord of Lords; and while the Beast and False 'Prophet shall be cast into

* Chap. xix.

a fiery lake, never to rise again, the carcases of the slain are described as exposed to the birds of prey on the great battlefield, and "all the birds are filled with their flesh."

It is only a childish adherence to the letter, or a dense incapacity to read off figures of speech, that can take this vision of the seer to mean a battle with carnal weapons, and a flight of horrid vultures to batten on corpses lying unburied in the open field. Moral conflicts, no doubt, have embodied themselves in actual martial strife, and may do so again; but that on which attention should be fixed is the awful fact of a vast combined opposition to the sway of the Lord Jesus Christ, and the certainty that this will involve the nations in sore punishment. Judgments, like the vultures, will rush from all quarters, and swoop down on the carcase of ungodly Antichristian society. There is a long time of patience, but it has its limit, and in the end the tares must be gathered in bundles and burnt, the carcase must be given up to the vultures.

Those birds do not touch the living. The

Christians were unhurt when Jerusalem fell. And so on the larger scale the hour of judgment to the adversaries of Christ will be not only a time of safety, but the very epoch of triumphant deliverance to His faithful followers. The signs of the end are to them tokens of redemption drawing nigh.

This does not mean that the Christian society or visible Church of the period will have nothing to fear. In so far as it may be found torn into factions and distracted like ancient Jerusalem in its last days, it cannot go unpunished. Only the living and the loving can be found of the Lord in peace at His appearing. For all others, even though they have had "a name to live," it will be a day of wrath. And no matter what the body has been, if it be a carcase, there will the vultures be gathered together.

III. *A reminder that our God is a God of judgment, and yet none the less a God of love.*

In nature He has made the ravenous beasts and birds, as well as those which are gentle and harmless. If the turtle-dove be His creature, so also is the raven, the hawk, or the vulture. If the lamb or the gazelle be His, so also are the wolf and the hyena. Nature has room and need for both mildness and severity. So has the government of the world. It requires and calls forth not merely the goodness and patience of the Supreme Ruler, but also His retributive justice, doing terrible things in righteousness. "It is written, Vengeance belongeth unto Me ; I will recompense, saith the Lord." * There is no need to assume an apologetic tone on this view of the Divine character and procedure. It is worthy of God so to mark His displeasure with corruptions of faith and life, and prevent the triumph of iniquity.

In all His severity God is love. That He has made birds of keen scent and piercing sight to fasten on carcases and remove decaying flesh is surely a proof of His care for the sweetness of the air and the health of living creatures. Vultures are not attractive—they are hideous ; but they do a service which birds of fair aspect and delicate appetite could not render ; their agency is for good.

* Romans xii. 19.

So there are calamities which are described as judgments of God falling on individuals and on communities during the present time of proof and discipline, and these will increase on the earth in the last days; but they must not be regarded as inconsistent with the goodness and loving-kindness of God. If He cared not for mankind, He would let their transgressions pass with impunity, and let all flesh go on unchecked to "corrupt their way before Him;" so would men infect one another with moral plagues, and the race would destroy itself by accumulating vice and violence. But God loves the world, and therefore He judges, and will judge it, in righteousness.

That it is more congenial to the Divine feeling to show mercy, who can doubt? The Lord has sworn by His own life that He has no pleasure in the death of sinners; and His long-suffering toward individuals and nations that proudly trespass against Him shows how reluctant He is to smite and to consume. But if men will persist in choosing death rather than life, they must surely die. If nations will not serve God and righteousness, they must come to nought. Justice requires, and even mercy dictates, that the eagles or vultures, far-sighted and strong-winged, be let loose upon the carcase. If not, the moral atmosphere would become heavy with corruption, and a plague would spread from which hardly any could escape.

The severity of God is not the opposite of His goodness, but its ally. It is He whose name is "Jehovah God, merciful and gracious," who "will by no means clear the guilty." It is He who has revealed His righteousness in the gospel for the salvation of sinners who has also revealed "wrath against all ungodliness and unrighteousness of men."

We anticipate no good result from the present-day tendency to avoid or soften statements of God's impending judgment. We trace its influence in superficial views of the guilt of sin and a feeble grasp of the great fact and doctrine of Atonement. Thinking, apparently, to make the gospel more credible and acceptable by dwelling solely on the parental love of God, many teachers are destroying the very foundations of the gospel, and sapping or weakening in the consciences of men anything like a serious conviction of their need of "so great salvation." We do not wish to revel in terrors; but it is cowardice, not charity, to know that they approach, and not sound an alarm. St. Paul is charitable enough for us; and he writes of "wrath and indignation, tribulation and anguish, upon every soul of man that worketh evil." *

* Romans ii. 9.

XXV.

HOUSE-SERVANTS.

"Watch therefore: for ye know not on what day your Lord cometh. But know this, that if the master of the house had known in what watch the thief was coming, he would have watched, and would not have suffered his house to be broken through. Therefore be ye also ready: for in an hour that ye think not the Son of Man cometh. Who then is the faithful and wise servant, whom his lord hath set over his household, to give them their food in due season? Blessed is that servant, whom his lord when he cometh shall find so doing. Verily I say unto you, that he will set him over all that he hath. But if that evil servant shall say in his heart, My lord tarrieth; and shall begin to beat his fellow-servants, and shall eat and drink with the drunken; the lord of that servant shall come in a day when he expecteth not, and in an hour when he knoweth not, and shall cut him asunder,

"Watch therefore: for ye know not when the lord of the house cometh, whether at even, or at midnight, or at cockcrowing, or in the morning; lest coming suddenly he find you sleeping. And what I say unto you I say unto all, Watch."—ST. MARK xiii. 35-37.

and appoint his portion with
the hypocrites: there shall be
the weeping and gnashing of
teeth."—St. Matt. xxiv. 42-51.

THE ancients divided the night into equal
periods, called watches, as marking the time
during which a sentinel might be kept on duty,
and at the end of which he ought to be relieved.
Originally the Jews made three watches of
four hours each, but afterwards adopted the
Roman system of four watches of three hours
each. This arrangement of time passed into
popular language in Judea and Galilee. It
was usual to speak of the watches of the
night, even though no guard or sentry stood
awake. We ourselves speak of an instrument
for measuring time as a watch; and when
one is awake to the lapse of time and has
his faculties on the alert, we say that he
watches or is on the watch.

The Lord Jesus compared Himself to the
master of a house who should go on a journey, and return at an uncertain hour of the
night or the morning. It would be the duty
of the servants in such a house to watch
for their master's coming. Now, whatever

was the impression on the minds of the apostles regarding the proximity of the Lord's return, His own prescient eye beheld a long stretch of time to elapse before His second advent, involving serious dangers of degeneracy, self-indulgence, and unseemly disputes 'among successive generations of His servants. Therefore He charged His disciples to watch. He enjoined and re-enjoined this, and the charge is repeated and urged by His apostles Peter and Paul, evidently as one which there would be a strong tendency to overlook or forget.

To watch in view of the coming of Christ is a comprehensive direction for an alert, well - braced, and well - employed Christian life. It means not a feverish expectation of one all-absorbing event, but calm and consistent adherence to the line of ascertained duty with a steady resistance to temptation, and all this actuated by the consideration that the Lord is at hand, and by the desire to be accepted and approved by Him at His glorious appearing.

In St. Matthew's report of our Lord's

sayings the illustration from a householder is put in two ways :—

1. In the first instance (vers. 42–44), the householder is supposed to have gone to rest in security ; but awaking, finds a robber in the house, or perhaps only sees the hole in the earthen wall through which the robber has escaped with his plunder. This is to illustrate the one point of the unexpectedness of the second advent. Not that even this point should be taken quite absolutely and universally. Vigilant spiritual minds will perceive signs of the nearness of the Son of Man ; but the world at large, even Christendom itself, will be taken by surprise. The suggestion of the thief in the night is not a pleasant one, but it is very telling for the point intended. No one who has had his house robbed at night can forget the amazement and chagrin with which he found in the morning that thieves had entered and escaped again while he slept. It is needless to say that there can be no intention here or in similar passages in the Book of Revelation * to liken any movement of the

* Chaps. iii. 3 ; xvi. 15.

Saviour to that of a wicked prowler in the night, save in the one point indicated. As St. Peter has it, "The day of the Lord shall so come as a thief in the night." It is approaching with muffled footsteps; it will be upon us while men sleep.

2. In the second form of the illustration (vers. 45–57) the householder has gone to a distant country, promising to return to his house, but not letting the steward or the servants know at what time he will arrive. It is for them to mind their work as though he were present, and to have everything in readiness for his return. In this case, the householder evidently represents Jesus Christ. The departure to a far country is His ascension to heaven. The return at an unknown hour is His second coming at an unknown date.

Emphasis is laid, according to St. Matthew, on the duty and responsibility of the steward; according to St. Mark, on the charge given to the porter at the gate. Such upper servants suggest the apostolate, and subsequently all authoritative and influential ministration in the Church. The ordinary servants represent Christian people at large ; and it is significant of the duty which our Lord expects every Christian to discharge that this householder gave to each of the servants "his work."   Not every one is to manage, not every one to take the lead, not every one to keep the gate ; but every one has his own place to fill and his own function to discharge for the absent Master.

The householder returns unannounced. How does he find the household ? Is the mansion in order ?   Is the prescribed work done ?   Do the servants stand with girt loins and lamps lit, while the porter opens the gate immediately ?   Or is the house a scene of riot and quarrel ? Is the steward the foremost in gluttony and drunkenness ?   Is the porter asleep ? Have the servants forgotten their Master and neglected their work ?

Such are the questions which ought to press on the Christian conscience during these long years of the. Saviour's withdrawal to heaven. We do not like to say His absence, because in the Spirit He is with us always.

But what is the effect of His unseenness and of the apparent delay of His coming on the officers of His Church and on Christian society at large? How would His servants be found if Christ should come before the cock crow to-morrow morning?

On this, as on most practical subjects, there are opposite extremes, between which the safe path lies.

1. There is an excess of feverish expectation. In some of those who love the Lord, and therefore love His appearing, there is a nervous, over-excited feeling about His advent. They are always occupied with what they take for a demonstration that the day of the Lord is actually at hand. Accordingly, they excuse themselves from attempting any arduous task or working towards any great practical reform, or even trying to bring the visible Church of God to any better order and harmony, on the ground that the Lord Himself is very near, and will set all things in order at His coming and His kingdom. So the Thessalonians were in a feverish mood about the

advent till the Apostle Paul wrote and charged them not to be shaken or troubled. So at various dates Christendom has been agitated and injured by illusive expectations. At such times it is as though the servants of the absent householder laid down their unfinished tasks and spent all their time looking out of the windows, because they felt sure that the master might be expected at any moment.   But what the householder required of them, and what Jesus Christ requires of His people, is that they work patiently, cheering their hearts at work by the hope of His return, so that they may be found ready for any further service or higher trust which He may assign to them at His coming.

2. The other extreme is more common. The lapse of time enfeebles the devotion to Christ which marked the primitive Church, and relaxes the sense of duty.   So the house, which ought to have been one of well-regulated activity and mutual kindness, has too often presented a spectacle of neglected duties, bitter quarrels, and raging controversies. Some

servants are stupefied with self-indulgence, and some are overcharged with cares of this life. These are neither working the works of God nor watching unto prayer. Some take to beating or persecuting others. At one time this was done with fire and sword, prison and torture. Nowadays it is done chiefly by the tongue and the pen and printing-press. The inward temper of hatred and intolerance is the same. Is this a scene on which one would like the Lord to descend, fixing His eyes as a flame of fire on such wicked servants? The severe language in which Jesus indicated the punishment which servants so misconducting themselves would receive from the householder, their master, ought to give pause to every one who calls Him Lord and Master, and so professes to be His servant. Woe to the in-tolerant and arrogant, and woe to the indolent and self-pampering Christians (most of all, to such officers of the Church) in that day !

The middle course is not a compromise, but a proper adjustment of the duties of waiting and working. He waits and watches best who works most diligently on the task which has been assigned to him. And for both watching and working he must avoid pampering of the flesh, burdens of worldly care, and all unseemly quarrels with his fellow-servants in the household of God.

It is the Old Testament which bids men work in view of death and "the grave whither thou goest." * The New Testament bids Christian men serve in view not of death and the grave so much as of their Master's return. Some say that practically this comes to the same thing. We think not. The expectation of Christ's coming and our gathering together to Him includes within it all that is useful in the expectation of death, and at the same time throws far more zest into our service and more brightness into our spirits. True, that many who lived and desired the Lord's appearing have not seen it, but have ended their course by dying. Many may still do so before He actually descends from heaven. The time is appointed by the Father, and not disclosed to any creature. But if it be appointed to us of this generation to die, as our

Eccles. ix. 10.

fathers have done, we have made no mistake: our waiting for the Lord is our best preparation for death. We wait in diligent service, in sober living, in brotherly kindness, and in prayer. What else, what more, should there be in order to meet death with safety and serenity?

An impression is abroad that if one only knew that death was near, he would and should wind up his affairs, see his lawyer, then his minister, read the Bible and good books, and resign himself to the inevitable; nay, even try to attune himself in some degree for a quite new life in heaven. But a wise Christian man should need no such special ado about dying. As to his affairs, he should have them so arranged that if any sudden stroke of death should remove him, no injury that he might have prevented shall befall others. Besides this, there is nothing to do but go on steadily with whatever work the Master has committed to him; and so abide in his calling, praying always—not "Come, O death!" or "Stay away!" but "Come, Lord Jesus!" So will the heart be prepared for

either the smaller event or the greater; and
fear of death will be swallowed up in the hope
of glory.

Two brief directions should be written on
every Christian conscience — Watch and be
sober; Watch and pray.

Watch and be sober! Not only abhor sur-
feiting and drunkenness, but beware of keen
ambition, exorbitant desire, and all excessive
worldly anxiety. We may not judge men
absolutely by outward appearance, for an inherited peculiarity of constitution sometimes
gives to a quite innocent person the aspect
of a glutton or a wine-bibber; but, allowance
being made for such exceptional cases, it does
pain us to see men who profess and call themselves Christians bearing on their figures and
countenances the marks of such indulgence of
appetite as stupefies the soul, or carrying about
a careworn face that tells of the unsatisfied
thirst for uncertain riches.

Watch and pray ! So said the Lord to the
disciples who slumbered in the garden of
Gethsemane; and · He added the significant
words, "That ye enter not into temptation."

Simon Peter, who was one of those disciples, combined the two counsels thus—"The end of all things is at hand : be ye therefore sober, and watch unto prayer." *

We do not dilate here on the deep sleep in which the world is sunk, its indifference to spiritual truth, and absolute sluggishness, of thought and feeling regarding God and the things of God. We lament the spirit of slumber in the Church. Alas! it is so easy to grow lethargic in Christian feeling and service; and this is a peril which haunts advanced Christians as well as those who are only beginners. Christian and Hopeful in the "Pilgrim's Progress" were far advanced before they reached the Enchanted Ground, *i.e.*, passed through a temptation to inglorious ease. Then Hopeful felt so drowsy that he could scarcely keep his eyes open, and besought Christian to lie down. "We may be re-freshed," he said, "if we take a nap." But the other reminded him how the shepherds had warned them of this enchanted ground, and also hinted that what might be intended

* 1 Peter iv. 7.

only to be a nap might prove a sleep of death. In the second part of the Allegory we see two men who had lain down to sleep for a little time in an arbour on that ground, but could never be waked again. The name of the one was Heedless; that of the other Too Bold.

XXVI.

THE TEMPLE.

"Jesus answered and said unto them, Destroy this temple, and in three days I will raise it up. The Jews therefore said, Forty and six years was this temple in building, and wilt thou raise it up in three days? But He spake of the temple of His body. When therefore He was raised from the dead, His disciples remembered that He spake this; and they believed the scripture, and the word which Jesus had said."—St. John ii. 19-22.

THIS metaphor was not dragged into the conversation, but was taken, according to our Lord's manner, from the incident and topic of the hour. Every one was astonished at the zeal and authority with which He had driven a sordid traffic from the courts of the temple. So He seized the opportunity to weave a deeper meaning into familiar words, and show the temple to be a figure of something greater and more sacred than itself.

While He used a metaphor, He at the same time put forth an enigma. It was not in-

R

frequent with Him to do so, for in this way He was able to cast a shadow for a time over truths, a full disclosure of which might have altered the conduct of the Jews towards Him and hindered the fulfilment of His mission. In the instance now before us He put His thought in a form that puzzled His hearers and excited after-thought. It was inexplicable to His own disciples till He had died and risen from the grave. To the rulers of the Jews His saying seemed to be a profanity. Destroy that magnificent building, on which the great Herod had lavished wealth and splendour, and in which the God of their fathers dwelt! And raise up in three days what had occupied skilled workmen for forty-six years! What good man could propose such a destruction? What sane man could promise such a restoration? At the same time they could not shake off the saying as an absurdity or impossibility. It lay in their memory, and, as their malignity towards the Saviour increased, it was preserved as an expression which might help to support a deadly accusation against Him. Accordingly we find it misquoted against Him in the high priest's palace, and, in the same inaccurate version of it, hurled at Him while He hung upon the cross.[*]

The Evangelist gives the clue to the Saviour's meaning. " He spake of the temple of His body."

There was more than metaphor here, or metaphor tipped with enigma; there was typical correspondence. The tabernacle in the wilderness and the successive temples in Jerusalem were divinely appointed signs, and, in theological phrase, types of an incarnate manifestation of God. If He deigned to dwell in a tent or a house of man's building, it was simply a condescension to the unreadiness of His people for a more spiritual conception of His presence, and a significant preparation for a time of more advanced privilege, when the Word which was God would become flesh and " tabernacle among men."

That Jesus Christ knew and proclaimed Himself to be the antitype to the temple reveals His consciousness of the fulness of

* St. Matt. xxvi. 60, 61 ; St. Mark xiv. 57, 58, xv. 29, 30.

the Godhead dwelling in Him bodily.* God
was in Him in a sense above that in which
He may be said to dwell in and reveal Himself
through all good and holy men ; for He was
in Christ by the mystery of the incarnation
and the hypostatical union of the Divine
nature with the human in one person. And
the temple which God thus provided was
by Him also consecrated; for Jesus was
anointed with the Holy Ghost and with
power.

Now the Lord foresaw clearly that the Jews
would destroy this temple. They who boasted
so much of a temple made with hands, as
though it could contain the High and Holy
One, were soon to reject, and, so far as their
power went, to rend and destroy the temple of
His body, which was the true meeting-place
with God. He was prepared for a violent
death, and was reconciled to it, nay, longed
to have it accomplished, because it would lead
to a glorious restoration. As He stood and
taught among the Jews, confined to a small

* Deity in bodily manifestation. See Bishop Lightfoot's
comment on Coloss. ii. 9.

spot of the earth and subject to many limitations of outward condition, He could not call to Himself all nations. The temple of His body must needs be destroyed in order to be rebuilt on a scale more glorious. In other words, He must be crucified in weakness in order to be raised in power.

The words " I will raise it again " are in two respects significant — (1.) As to the identity of the body in which Christ rose with that in which He suffered. No doubt the transformation was great. The conditions of an incorruptible body are not known to us; but they must be very different from those of ordinary flesh and blood. We cannot tell how far it is ponderable, what are its laws of motion, or whether it is liable to waste, and if so, how the waste is repaired. But, as our Lord said of the body in which He stood before the Jews, that He would raise it again, there must be a link of continuity and identity between the mortal body and the immortal. And if there is such a link in the case of Christ, so also will there be in the case of all the saints, who are to have their bodies made like to His at the resurrection. They will be the same bodies as slept in the grave, yet purged of gross materials and fleshly appetites, unmolested by passion, exempt from disease, and guaranteed against decay. (2.) As to the power which our Saviour felt that He had over His own future. The usual statement is that God the Father raised Him up on the third day; but in the instance now before us, His authority to cleanse the temple had been called in question; and therefore He took occasion to say that He had power not only to purify a temple which men had built, but also to raise up a temple which men might destroy but could not construct, and to do it in three days.*

It is as He is risen, and in the power of His resurrection, that Jesus Christ is a temple for all nations. In Him God dwells, and is accessible to all. Neither at Jerusalem nor at Gerizim, nor at any holy city or holy mount, is it required that men assemble to worship God; for they may anywhere draw near to Him in Christ, and be at peace.

* Compare St. John x. 18.

Here is the place for reconciliation, and the home of communion, the refuge for sinners, and the resort of saints; a temple that will never be subverted and never crumble to decay—" Jesus Christ, the same yesterday, and to-day, and for ever."

With the light of the apostolic writings to guide us, we carry this vein of thought and illustration farther still. St. Paul thought of every individual Christian as a temple of God. Though he be in a mortal body, he has within him the power of an endless life—" the Holy Ghost which is in you." The inference is that sin is not to be served in that mortal body, and that its members are not to be "yielded as instruments of unrighteousness." Much has been said by moralists of the native dignity of man and the elevating power of self-respect, but St. Paul strikes a higher note and brings a stronger persuasion to bear on conscience and heart when he shows the relation to God and to Christ into which the very body of a Christian believer is brought. "Your bodies are members of Christ." "Know ye not that your body is a temple of the Holy Ghost, which is in you, which ye have from God ?" *

More frequently, however, the apostles represent individual believers as living stones, which form collectively a living temple. Thus the whole Church, which is the mystical body of Christ, is the temple, or "habitation of God in the Spirit." A local or particular Church, so far as its bounds extend, is the representative of the Church catholic, and is called a temple of God. So it was at Corinth, at Ephesus, and among the Christian Jews of the Eastern dispersion. †

The life which animates the living stones and so pervades the temple, emanates from the living foundation-stone, the risen Christ; but this cannot in the present time be made fully manifest. Just as the Lord Himself was not understood in Jerusalem, the Church is not now understood in the world, nor does it appear as it shall be. Christians are seen in poor mortal bodies, but their inner life is not seen. So men look on Christian society

* 1 Cor. vi. 15, 19.
† See 1 Cor. iii. 16 ; Eph. ii. 21, 22 ; 1 Peter ii. 5.

and the forms in which it has organised itself, but do not discern the Lord's body. They survey Church buildings and institutions, but do not recognise the one spiritual edifice, the holy house of living stones.

Whether men recognise it sufficiently or not, Christ continues to build His Church in the power of His resurrection, so that the gates of Hades cannot prevail against it. He is still raising it up as the days go on, employing, as a Master-builder, many work-men, skilled and unskilled, upon the structure.

In such a world as this, a holy temple must needs encounter risk. As the cattle-dealers and money-changers desecrated the courts of the Lord's house at Jerusalem, so do men with a Christian name but a worldly heart secularise and degrade the Church of God. Such men, sooner or later, the Lord will drive out and disown. But greater still is the fault of those who by strife and schism tend to destroy the temple. They strike the pickaxes of contention into the wall, produce separations with a light heart; and, so

far as they succeed in loosening one stone
from another, they weaken and endanger the
entire structure. The whole process of sec-
tarian disintegration tends to convert the
Church into a heap of confusion, or rather
to form separate heaps of loose stones instead of "a building of God." Against this
St. Paul has lifted a stern warning—"If any
man destroy the temple of God, him shall
God destroy." * And the destroyers, in his
view, were not the persecutors of the Christians, but those Christians who said, "I am
of Paul, I of Apollos, I of Cephas," and so
set up rival parties and fostered separatism
in the Church of God.

To secularise the Church is to strike at
its holiness; and "holiness becometh Thine
house, O Lord, for ever." To split up the
Church is to strike at its life and peace. It
is to contradict the prayer — "Peace be
within thy walls, and prosperity within thy
palaces!"

* 1 Cor. iii. 17.

XXVII.

THE BREEZE.

" The wind bloweth where it listeth, and thou hearest the voice thereof, but knowest not whence it cometh, and whither it goeth ; so is every one that is born of the Spirit."—St. John iii. 8.

One who feels uneasy at the course which a conversation unexpectedly takes not infrequently tries to check or turn it by a puzzling question or a jest. So the Pharisee who came to discuss the claims of Jesus as a prophet, and opened with a large admission on the subject, was embarrassed by the Nazarene's reply, which did not at all follow his lead, but referred to the necessity of regeneration ; and to escape from or cover his embarrassment, Nicodemus put forward a question which was neither witty nor wise about the possibility of a man being born twice of his mother.

We at once see the ineptitude of this ; yet

we do not see much farther than Nicodemus did into the rationale of the birth from above. The origin of life is as much as ever veiled from human view; and if it be so in the springing of corn, the propagation of flowers, the multiplication of insects, and the quickening and birth of children, much more is there mystery about a spiritual life, originating within or communicated to one who already has physical, intellectual, and to some extent moral life and sensibility.

That there is something in the process of regeneration which we cannot see or explain is what natural analogies teach us to expect, but is no ground whatever for scepticism as to its possibility and reality. Jesus Christ, who "knew what was in man," has assured us that a man may be born again, and that the power which effects such a change is that of the Holy Spirit. Not only so. He has said that a man must be born again in order to enter into, or even to discern, the kingdom of God. And this evidently is no merely arbitrary 'condition laid down by authority; it rests on the very nature of the kingdom as spiritual, and therefore cognisable by none but spiritual minds. On the possibility and necessity of regeneration the authority of the Lord Jesus seems to us conclusive. As to its reality, we are satisfied by daily facts which any fair observer of Christian society may verify. Men are inwardly and completely changed. They take a new tone of character. They begin a fresh life like little children. They love what they used to hate, and hate what they used to love. Their disposition and conduct show that they "have received the Spirit which is of God."

The point which is brought into prominence by Christ's saying about the breeze is the unaccountableness of the regenerate or spiritual life to those who judge after the flesh. It was a point quite new to Nicodemus, for he, as a Pharisee and ruler of the Jews, had been trained in a religion of traditionalism and prescription, which allowed of no liberty, and was not merely very visible, but ostentatiously so, seeking glory from men.

Not improbably the metaphor was suggested

at the moment. It was evening, and after sunset a light breeze often springs up in such climates as that of Judea. If it happened so, and the breeze made itself felt or heard through the lattice during the Pharisee's visit, our Lord, according to His wont, seized on the passing incident to elucidate and impress His meaning. He used not the ordinary word for the wind (ὁ ἄνεμος), but that which means the breath, and is also rendered spirit (τὸ πνεῦμα). The suggestion is not of a whistling wind, but of the gentle breeze that rises and falls, comes and goes one knows not how; and not of stormy darkness, but rather of a night

"When the sweet wind did gently kiss the trees."

That the metaphor was suggested in this way we only put forth as a probable conjecture. With more certainty we trace it to Old Testament Scripture, with which the mind of Jesus was so richly stored. The passage which, as we suppose, was in His view, runs thus :— "As thou knowest not what is the way of the spirit, nor how the bones do grow in the womb of her that is with child, even so thou knowest not the works of God who maketh all." * The play of the light wind and the mystery of the living babe unborn are joined together as things which are known and yet cannot be defined.

Often this saying to Nicodemus is quoted as though it made the breeze an illustration of the movement and action of the Holy Spirit. But what our Lord spoke of was the way which they take, the liberty they exercise, who are born of the Spirit.

In modern times we trace the path of the winds and measure their strength and velocity. We try to reach the general laws which govern those currents of air. We know that, like all the forces in nature, they are under control, and are enclosed in the comprehensive plan and order of creation ; and yet, so far as man's control is concerned, the wind is a thing of unchained liberty, and gives to us small account of its coming and going. The operation of the Holy Spirit, in like manner, is according to the law of God's

* Eccles xi. 5. Spirit or inspiring breath. The Septuagint has πνεῦμα.

new creation, and is enclosed in His comprehensive purpose of grace, but does not submit itself to human judgment or control. It goes forth as a Divine breath with a sovereignty that silences questions and defies curiosity. But not only so. As is the Spirit of God, so are they who are born of the Spirit. The Spirit is holy, and they follow after holiness. The Spirit is free, and they walk in liberty. It is hard for those who are inured to a religion of prescription and constraint to credit that freedom is either holy or safe; but it is none the less a " doctrine according to godliness " that Christ makes Christians "free indeed."

The vast majority of men are easily accounted for; they are copies of each other. In the same community they think the same thoughts, form the same habits, entertain the same prejudices, repeat the same sentiments, and in the same phrases. There is no mystery about them. We become familiar with the type of man who belongs to this set or to that profession, and understand whence he came and whither he goes. Only at rare intervals do we fall in with one who is really fresh and individual, and of whom we cannot predicate what he will say and do, whence his thoughts and convictions come, and whither they tend.

Even in Christian circles, where familiarity with the most momentous and profound matters ought to deepen and strengthen character, there is much vapid commonplace. Men copy religion from one another, put on the same form of godliness, set up the same conventional standard of virtue, use the same phrases and signs of devotion. Nay, when they are most in earnest they are so at second hand, catching a sort of contagious zeal from others. We have no difficulty in seeing whence their religion comes and whither it goes. It has no secret source, no hidden strength, no contact of heart with God. But there should be something unique about every one that is born of the Spirit. He is one of a holy society; but he has not been born of the society : he is of God.

A worldly-wise mind is very apt to misjudge such a man. At all events, it is puzzled by him, and asks, Whence comes this enthusiasm? What makes this man so fond of the Bible and of the Church? Are his nerves shaken? Is his brain touched? Or is he a shrewd schemer who makes gain out of assumed godliness? And whither will this go? How will it reach its limit? When and where will it stop?

A mind that can discern spiritual things perceives this much about the life of godliness, that it comes from a hidden heavenly source, and goes on to an unseen heavenly issue. It has been well said by a modern Oxford divine, " The destination of the character of the man of the world, even if he is respectable and in his own way useful, is not an invisible one; all his qualities are obviously made for this world as their field of exercise; they do not point to or give any forecast of another. But the character which has the unknown origin is itself a prophecy and presage of another world, because it seems made for it. Its source and its destination then are alike beyond our sight. We do not see that great Spirit from whom the sons of God derive their birth; we do not see that heavenly society towards which they are journeying. Whence they come and whither they go we see not; and that because they are born of the Spirit." *

The great perplexity which filled the minds of men regarding our Lord Jesus Himself was, Whence had He come? and Whither did He go? Whence had He derived such wisdom, authority, and power? Certainly not from Nazareth. And whither did He tend? What did He mean by going to His Father? He was inexplicable because He was so spiritual, so heavenly. With His disciples, indeed, He was at pains to expound the mystery of His origin and destiny. He showed them plainly that He had come from God, and would return to God. Nicodemus thought that He knew at least the first half of this, viz., that Jesus was "a teacher come from God." But he needed to be born again in order to apprehend clearly whence and why Jesus had come, and whither He would go. "Whither I go ye know, and the way ye know."

* Mozley's University Sermons, p. 242.

The true followers of Christ are, like Himself, heaven-born and heaven-tending. Therefore the world knows them not. Therefore, too, they are a wonder to themselves—a wonder of Divine compassion and grace. And therefore, too, they are bound to be brotherly and forbearing one toward another. The breeze demands freedom, and so does the Spirit-born life in man. So soon as a Christian man understands this, he ceases to dictate to his brother, or to set up in the Church mere conventional tests and laws of uniformity.

It is death that is formal, measured, and monotonous. It has no breath, no feeling, no movement. Life must have liberty. It moves like the breeze; and the higher the quality of the life, the more the scope which it requires for its activities. This will seem to religious pedants full of risk. They will urge that freedom is apt to be abused and to degenerate into license; and that men who are capricious, or perhaps obstinate, may represent to others, and even persuade themselves, that they are following the guidance of the Divine Spirit, when they are really actuated by fickle fancy or pertinacious self-will. It may be so. Be it so: nevertheless liberty is the heritage of the children of God, and it is not to be denied to them because by some who are ill instructed it may be misconstrued or misused. We must not be entangled again in any yoke of bondage. In the Spirit we may have great boldness of speech, stretch of faith, flow of affection, inspiration of hope, insight into truth, and outgoings of the soul to things which eye has not seen nor ear heard. We do not want more straps and buckles to pinch and squeeze our life. We want more life. We want to breathe more freely, and so to exhale what we inhale. We want to drink more deeply of the living water, and so to give forth freely rivers of living water. Come freely, O quickening Breath! Flow freely, O living and life-inspiring Stream!

XXVIII.

LIVING WATER.

" Jesus answered and said unto her, If thou knewest the gift of God, and who it is that saith to thee, Give Me to drink ; thou wouldest have asked of Him, and He would have given thee living water. The woman saith unto Him, Sir, thou hast nothing to draw with, and the well is deep: from whence then hast thou that living water ? Art thou greater than our father Jacob, which gave us the well, and drank thereof himself, and his sons, and his cattle? Jesus answered and said unto her, Every one that drinketh of this water shall thirst again: but whosoever drinketh of the water that I shall give him shall never thirst; but the water that I shall give him shall become in him a well of water springing up unto eternal life. . . . Now on the last day, the great day of the feast, Jesus stood and cried, saying, If any man thirst, let him come unto Me, and drink. He that believeth on Me, as the Scripture hath said, out of his belly shall flow rivers of living water. But this spake He of the Spirit, which they that believed on Him were to receive : for the Spirit was not yet given ; because Jesus was not yet glorified."— ST. JOHN iv. 10-14 ; vii. 37-39.

IN each of the Scriptures quoted above we have a beautiful instance of the felicity with which Jesus Christ turned the incident of the moment to spiritual use and found sacred metaphors in familiar things. Nothing could have been more natural or unstudied than

His behaviour at the well of Sychar. It was what any wayworn traveller might have done, to rest at such a spot, and to ask for a drink from the first comer, as He carried no vessel with Him, and the well was deep. But then came into exercise His unique faculty for speaking "a word in season;" and the seat by the well became a chair of Divine philosophy, or a pulpit of godly instruction, while He talked of living water. The second instance was at Jerusalem, and on the last or eighth day, the great day of the Feast of Booths. According to custom, water was drawn from the pool of Siloam and poured out in the court of the temple, while trumpets sounded and the air was rent with joyful acclamations. Jesus, being present, saw His opportunity to proffer to the people a blessing fraught with more lasting joy. So He stood and cried, "If any man thirst, let him come to Me, and drink."

It is characteristic of the fourth Evangelist that this metaphor, omitted in the other Gospels, has been noted and preserved by him. His mind was much occupied with the thought of eternal life in Christ, and with the persuasion that the Father had given power to the Son to quicken whom He would. Accordingly, it is in his Gospel that we read of the gift of life, light of life, water of life, bread of life, and resurrection of life.

To take water as an emblem of spiritual vitality was not an original suggestion in the sense of being absolutely new. Poets and prophets of Judah had referred to fountains and streams in the same metaphorical manner. Isaiah wrote the often-quoted words, "With joy shall ye draw water out of the wells of salvation. * In Jeremiah Jehovah had described Himself as "the fountain of living waters." †

These Scriptures, however, were unknown to the woman at Sychar, for the Samaritans received only the Pentateuch. Even had she known them, it is not likely that she would have caught their inner sense. A woman of her habits could not readily pass into the grave sweet idealism of the prophetic soul.

* Isa. xii. 3. See also Isa. xli. 17, 18.　　† Jer. ii. 13.

See how she was puzzled by the Saviour's mention of living water. Water that is not stagnant is living. It bubbles in a fountain or flows in a stream. The water of the well at Sychar was living, and the well itself was of great fame. All the citizens were proud of it; the more so' that they traced it back to one whom they held in high honour, their ancestor Jacob. What could this stranger mean by alleging that he could give living water, better in quality than she could draw from Jacob's well? Still, if He could in any way relieve her of the daily drudgery which she had to perform in coming out to this spot and carrying her large jar of water on her head into the town, she would be glad to know how He proposed to do it. He evidently spoke not in jest; but the thing was too good to be true.

The Lord spoke in a figure both at Sychar and at Jerusalem. Under the name of living water He indicated some element which is indispensable to the welfare of the inner man, and has power to refresh and nourish that life which is everlasting.

He Himself is the true well or fountain of that life. In Him all fulness dwells, and out of His fulness we receive. Whosoever wishes to obtain living water must ask it of Him. Whosoever is athirst is to come to Him and drink. And what a wonderful thought is this! What a claim to be made by a "carpenter's son" from Nazareth! It was either an unpardonable exaggeration or it is a witness to the conscious Divinity as well as humanity of our Saviour. Is it conceivable that any one with an honest heart and a reverence for truth would presume, while knowing himself to be only a man, to present himself to all mankind and say, "Come to Me and drink!" Is it credible that a devout man of the Hebrew race, acquainted with the books of the prophets, would, even if he knew himself to be a prophet like Isaiah or Jeremiah, have presumed to point to himself as being what Jehovah had proclaimed Himself to be, "the fountain of living waters"? It is not conceivable, not credible. This man must have been more than man; this prophet

was more than a prophet. Truly this was
the Son of God.

The water drawn from Christ as the well is
the Spirit of Life which He imparts. It is
not easy to express in words the connection
between the Divine Son and the Divine Spirit
in personal salvation and experience ; but
there is no real perplexity or confusion, as
serious Christians well know. That Christ is
with us always is explained by the abiding
of the Spirit. Christ quickens us by impart-
ing the Spirit of Life, and lives in us by
His Spirit dwelling within us. Indeed, if we
dwell in love, we dwell in God, and He in us.*
But in so far as the relation of the Divine
Son and of the Divine Spirit to the individual
believer may be distinguished in a figure, the
illustration now before us is perhaps the most
apposite that can be found. The well represents Jesus Christ, the Prince of Life.

> " O Christ ! He is the fountain,
> The deep sweet well of love."

Then the water or element of life, which
Christ freely imparts, is the Spirit of all grace,

* 1 John iv. 16.

which we receive. We are "all made to drink into one Spirit."

The points of analogy are obvious:—(1.) As the well at Sychar was free to all comers, so is Jesus Christ free and accessible to all. The invitation by the pen of the prophet Isaiah holds good—" Ho! every one that thirsteth, come ye to the waters, and he that hath no money."* Water is often sold in the Eastern cities to those who have money, but the public well is for all, "without money and without price." (2.) As water is a necessary of life, and has power to enliven the faint and refresh the weary, so is the Holy Spirit necessary to the interior life of faith and prayer, and able both to restore the discouraged and to revive the languid and the sorrowful.

It is a point of contrast on which our Lord laid emphasis at Sychar. He reminded the Samaritan woman that water from Jacob's well, or any similar source, would give but a temporary relief from thirst. He who drank of it soon needed to drink again; and for

* Isaiah lv. 1.

the simple reason, that the water imbibed is soon worked off or consumed in the constant waste of the vital system. But it is not so with the living water which Jesus Christ is able to give; it is not spent or exhausted in the operation of the spiritual life. Thus the Holy Ghost, when received, abides. A follower of Jesus does indeed desire and pray for a more copious supply of the Spirit; but he is not without the Spirit, and ought not to feel or to pray as though he had yet for the first time to taste that living water.

See how we have to do with the objective and the subjective Christ—Christ without and Christ within. As the woman of Sychar had to go out of her house, and even beyond the gate of the town, to reach the well and draw water, so every one who would obtain living water must go beyond himself, his house, his whole social and moral environment, and come to Jesus Christ as He is revealed in the gospel, full of grace and truth. This application to Him in faith must go first. Then follows a marvellous thing. Christ enters into the heart that has "asked of Him." He dwells in the heart by faith. Thus there is not only water, but a well of water in "the inner man." St. Paul said truly, "Christ liveth in me." From the well or indwelling Christ the waters gush. His Spirit actuates the thoughts, desires, words, and actions of each living Christian. The whole outflow from the seat of inner life is good and holy. Out of the spiritual man "flow rivers of living water."

There may be—there ought to be—increase of faith, and so of spiritual life. The inward well may be deepened, and the stream which issues from it may have a more copious flow. Alas! the opposite too often occurs. The well may be half choked with rubbish and the rivers all but dried up by worldliness. Still the rule is continuance; the thing expected is the steady spiritual life secured by the indwelling Christ and His abiding Spirit.

The career of the man Christ Jesus was a consummate example of life in the Spirit. And how strong was the current of this life and power in Him is shown by the holy zeal with which He forgot His own physical want when the opportunity came to Him of opening spiritual things to one Samaritan listener. So far as we learn, He drank not at all of Jacob's well; and when His disciples brought food to Him from the town, they heard Him say that He had meat to eat that they knew not of. Then the woman also, beginning to feel the pulsations of a new life, forgot the purpose for which she had come out to that spot, left her water-pot at the well, and hastened into the town to call the people to the Christ. She compares favourably with Nicodemus under very similar instruction. When the Pharisee had heard of "water and the Spirit," he departed as he had come, under the cover of night—"secretly, for fear of the Jews." But this woman went openly and spoke to the men of her city regarding Jesus. She might have been deterred by fear of them. Her manner of life exposed her to reproach. She might be jeered at bitterly, as a strange person to turn missionary. But she cared not what men might say of her. Let them only come to the Man who had told her all things that ever she did!

Some persons are sceptical of great spiritual changes, and view the doctrine of a Divine indwelling as a sort of " tall talk " in religion. We do not attempt to prove such things by argument to persons who themselves have no more than a form of godliness and deny its power.   Intellectual demonstrations can be made to those only who have a sufficient intellectual aptitude and preparation for them. In like manner spiritual phenomena can be made plain and certain to those only who, knowing the power of godliness, are able to discern and estimate the operation of that power on others.   No person who has himself experienced the quickening grace of the Holy Spirit doubts the transforming operation of that Spirit on others, or has difficulty in believing that God now dwells with men. There are Christian lives to be seen every day by those who have eyes to see which evidently are no mere surface amendments of conduct, but have a pervading tone and a deep motive force that come from God.   They do not proceed on mere impulse, and are not sustained by human encouragement or applause.   Often those who lead such lives have to endure discouragement and obloquy; yet they continue fresh, lively, resolute, patient, and fruitful. It is because there is a well of water within—such water as springs up to life everlasting.

Happy they who have Christ in their hearts, and all the outflow of whose character is actuated and hallowed by His Spirit! A Christian who has no experience of this hardly deserves that name. When you visit the ruins of ancient castles and strongholds, you are pretty sure to find an old well in the courtyard, perhaps choked up and dry, perhaps still yielding living water. Weak would the fortress have been, however thick its walls and brave its garrison, if it had no fountain within itself providing a supply of water that no enemy could cut off. So with the fortress of " Mansoul." It can stand no siege, endure no hardness, make no long resistance to assault, unless within it, guarded and cherished, there be a well of living water, a fountain of strength, wisdom, purity, and comfort, and a continual supply of the Spirit of Christ Jesus.

T

XXIX.

LIVING BREAD.

" Work not for the meat which perisheth, but for the meat which abideth unto eternal life, which the Son of Man shall give unto you: for Him the Father, even God, hath sealed. . . . I am the bread of life. Your fathers did eat the manna in the wilderness, and they died. This is the bread which cometh down out of heaven, that a man may eat thereof, and not die. I am the living bread which came down out of heaven: if any man eat of this bread, he shall live for ever: yea, and the bread which I will give is My flesh, for the life of the world."—St. John vi. 27, 48-51.

This metaphor, like so many more, was suggested by the occasion. There were two suggestions, and, following these, the truth which our Lord desired to inculcate received a growing expression.

I. In the first instance, a multitude had followed Jesus across the Lake of Galilee, because He had, on the previous day, fed them on barley-bread and fish in a desert place, and they hoped that He would do so again. They were poor people, and a gratuitous meal, even of the plainest food, was an object to them. It was not a very noble motive, but it was quite as good as that which influences a good many people now-a-days to value Jesus Christ for temporal benefits which they receive by attaching themselves to His Church, or for the inward satisfaction and comfort which they enjoy as Christians.

But Jesus Christ had not come to suspend the old law that by the sweat of his brow man must eat bread. Therefore He gave no encouragement to the hope which had drawn the multitude after Him, but began to speak to them of a better bread which He would give— food that would endure to eternal life. The case is exactly parallel to that of His conversation with the woman at Sychar, where He left off speaking of the water from Jacob's well, and set far above it the water that He could give as the element of a life everlasting.

It is also a point worthy of notice that in this instance, as also in that, the Lord dwelt not so much on the mystic element at the beginning of the conversation as on His own power to bestow it. He turned the thought of the Samaritan woman to Himself. If she had known Him, she would have asked of Him, and He would have given her living water. So also at Capernaum, He spoke to the people of Himself as able to give the food of an everlasting life. The mode, however, in which He described the necessary application to Him for the boon was significantly altered.. The woman should simply have asked. This multitude were told to work.

They liked this expression; it quite suited their conception of religion; and so, without a question about the nature of this mystic food, they asked for definite direction about the labour necessary for obtaining it. The Scribes and Pharisees had taught them on this wise—"This ye must do, and that ye must not do." What would the new Rabbi prescribe? "What shall we do that we may work the works of God?" But the reply of Jesus soon showed that He was not going to be a teacher of self-righteousness. "This is the work of God, that ye believe on Him whom He hath sent."

The question rises here—If our Lord meant "believe," why did He say "labour"? And divines jealous for the doctrine of free grace have been more at a loss for an answer than they need have been. They have gravely taught on this saying of Christ that men should "labour to get an appetite for spiritual meat," and have towards this object given such advices as the following:—That men should labour daily to discern what state they are in without Christ; that they should consider the vanity of those things that draw them from Christ; that they should "exercise themselves in resisting temptations and snares of Satan, so that the exercise may create an appetite in the soul;" and that they should reflect how soon the table Christ has spread may be taken away, "to the end that they may not neglect it any longer." * Very good admonitions, no doubt, but not very elucidative of the text. Christ said not labour for an appetite, but "labour for the meat." The

* See Dr. Richard Sibb's Works, vol. iii. pp. 359-361, ed. 1809.

meaning and the propriety of the phrase are
easily recognised if we attend to the occasion
on which it was used.   The woman at Sychar
had come out to the well to draw water, and
the Lord told her that by asking she might
draw from Him living water.   But the crowd
at Capernaum had come to that place by toil-
ing across the sea in small boats, seeking
Jesus.   This had been their labour for the
meat that perishes, because they hoped that
He would feed them again as He had done on
the previous evening.   So He told them to
take the same course for a better bread.   They
should spare no pains, lose no time, in seeking
the Son of Man, and applying to Him who
alone can give the food of the life everlasting ;
" for Him hath God the Father sealed."   Thus
the labour has nothing whatever in common
with the toils of self-righteousness.   It is in
sharp contrast with these ; for it is just the
earnest seeking of Jesus Christ till we find
Him, and applying to Him for what is not
our desert, but His free gift.   And what is
this but believing on Him whom God has
sent ?

So far the first stage of this teaching. The meaning of the spiritual bread was not disclosed, but it was revealed that such bread was obtainable; that in value it is as far above "barley loaves" as eternal life is above temporal; and that it is to be got by any and by all who, with minds intent upon it, repair to Jesus Christ.

II. As the conversation proceeded, the doctrine of the living bread from heaven came out more distinctly and emphatically. The opportunity for it was afforded by the language of the people. They understood our Saviour to hint at some bread superior to that of common life; and, jealous for the honour of "Moses in whom they trusted," as the Samaritan woman had been jealous for the honour of "our father Jacob," they recalled the days when their fathers, under the leadership of the great prophet-legislator, "ate manna in the wilderness." Jesus at once accepted the reference. Nothing could have been better for the elucidation of His doctrine.

He at once lifted the subject above any discussion of the power of Moses. The manna had been the gift of God, whom He claimed as His own Father. It had been immeasurably beyond the capacity of Moses to have given even one day's supply of bread to the twelve tribes. Then He showed that the manna itself, invaluable as it had been for its purpose, was not God's highest gift of bread. It was a sign of a better, or rather of a best, as the water in Jacob's well might be taken as the figure of a better, or rather of a best. The manna was a food that perished. It was peculiarly perishable,* and the generation that ate of it died as other generations had done. But now God had given from heaven a Living Bread, of which if a man should eat he would live for ever. The Bread of which He spoke, what was it? It was the Lord Himself, given by the Father—Bread that had "come down out of heaven."

The metaphor of receiving wisdom as by a process of eating and drinking was not new to those of our Lord's hearers who knew the Book of Proverbs—"Come, eat of my

* Exod. xvi. 20, 21.

bread, and drink of the wine which I have mingled." * There is a parallel passage in Ecclesiasticus,† and indeed the figure was frequently used by Jewish teachers, and is familiar to the Eastern mind. But Jesus Christ claimed to give more than wisdom. He bestowed everlasting life.

And how? Recognise here again, as well as in the metaphor of the well of water, the sequence of the objective Christ and the subjective Christ—the Bread for us provided by God and the Bread in us received and appropriated by faith. The Bread divinely given and sent from heaven is shown to us in the gospel. We see it and hail it with joy. We have spent our money for that which is not bread, but this requires no money or price. A voice from heaven says, "Hearken diligently unto Me, and eat ye that which is good." ‡ So we desist from our own desires, and, under the warrant of the Divine invitation and command, take freely what the God of love has freely bestowed. We believe, and believing we eat

* Prov. ix. 5.　　† Chap. xxiv. 18-21.　　‡ Isaiah lv. 2.

the Heavenly Bread. It enters into us; then all is changed. We have received and appropriated Jesus Christ, and He is now in us the staff and strength of a life which is everlasting. Indeed, all are dying men who are without this Bread. Only those live to God and are beyond the bitterness of death who have received the Lord Jesus to dwell in their hearts by faith.

Great ingenuity has been displayed by a certain school of divines in enumerating points of correspondence or coincidence between the manna and the True Bread which is Christ. Witsius gives twenty-six; but it is more profitable to ourselves, as well as more consonant with the dignity of the subject, to let the mind rest on a few simple and strong analogies. Thus:—(1.) In each case a Divine provision is made for human want, and made both copiously and freely. (2.) In each instance the free gift profits those only who receive it and take it home. The manna was free to every Israelite for the support of his life; but he must needs gather it within assigned limits of time, and carry it into his tent. So Christ is free to every man in order to an eternal life, but profits only those who receive Him within "the accepted time," and take Him to their homes and to their hearts. (3.) The manna was a daily bread, yielding a continuous nourishment. So Christ is, in an ineffable manner, a continuous spiritual bread, through the habitual action of faith. Christians live day after day by each day's faith in the Son of God.

The first gift of manna bread was accompanied by a supply of "flesh" in the wilderness. Jehovah gave this announcement through His servant Moses — "At even ye shall eat flesh, and in the morning ye shall be filled with bread." * Probably it was the recollection of this which led our Saviour to speak at Capernaum of flesh as well as bread. He showed that both were fulfilled in Him — "The bread is My flesh." Here He went farther than the metaphor of the well of water allowed Him to go at Sychar. He indicated the offering of Himself in sacrifice

* Exod. xvi. 12.

"for the life of the world." He is the Bread which sustains the everlasting life of believers, forasmuch as He was slain for them, and now lives as one who has passed through death, and dies no more.

This farther development of the metaphor puzzled the multitude. They asked, half in horror, half in ridicule, how "this Man" could give His own flesh to them to eat? What strange doctrine of cannibalism was this?

Superstition gives an explanation which neither our Lord nor any of His apostles so much as hinted at. It assumes that Christ referred to the Last Supper. No wonder, if so, that the people could not understand His teaching, as they could not have known any thing of an ordinance which was yet in the future. And then it breaks away from figure and metaphor altogether. It takes a piece of actual bread, and supposes it, while unchanged in its appearance and qualities, to be really transmuted into the actual body of Jesus Christ. Then this wonderful substance is received by the mechanical process of swallowing, and so a mystic sacramental grace is conveyed to the soul. But, as Dean Stanley has well said, "to suppose that the material can of itself reach the spiritual is not religion, but magic:" * and the dogma of transubstantiation is no answer at all to the question of eating the flesh and drinking the blood of the Son of Man. It is a doctrine of magic, not of godly faith. It outrages common sense, insults reason, contradicts the evidence of four of the five senses of mankind, and at the same time breaks every rule of consistent interpretation, confuses the material with the spiritual, and degrades the sublime truth of our Lord's *unition* with His people by faith into a mechanical action of the mouth and gullet.

We turn from superstition to that Christian Rationalism which is a reaction from it, and which spreads under the fine title of "Broad Church tendencies." This takes a practically Socinian view of the mission and work of Jesus Christ. He was a Divine Man,

---

* Christian Institutions, p. 107. We regret, however, to say that the chapter on "The Body and Blood" in this interesting volume is very unsatisfactory.

a profound Teacher, and a perfect Exemplar of virtue. But we ask any one to explain to us, on this theory, how this Man can give us His flesh to eat. Is not the saying paradoxical? Is it not even presumptuous? What meaning can there be in a man, however good and wise, being bread from heaven for the everlasting life of his fellow-men, or giving his flesh for the life of the world? The rationalistic theory has no answer. It has much to say about the admirable precepts of Jesus; but over this sublime revelation of Himself and His relation to the life of the world it is perplexed. For our part, we are quite persuaded that only the doctrine of the hypostatic union of divinity and humanity in the person of Christ taken with the doctrine of His sacrificial death can explain or justify such words as He uttered in the synagogue of Capernaum. Happy they who are firmly established in these truths, and who, alike in reading or hearing the Word and in observing the Lord's Supper, receive Jesus Christ into their hearts by faith with thanksgiving!

Sometimes one may find a ghastly and perverted shadow of sacred truth among the credulous notions and cruel customs of the heathen. Among many tribes it has been held that to drink the blood of a brave man will make one brave, and to eat the heart of a hero, though an enemy, will make one strong and daring. Hence many hideous orgies after battle between savages.

Such is the coarse carnal conception of the transfusion of one life into another. For the ends which a Christian life contemplates, we have the Lord's authority for saying that "the flesh profits nothing." The words which He spoke at Capernaum were spirit and life. What He imparts for eternal life can be received through the spiritual organs only, acting according to His Word. So Christians are partakers of Christ, but partakers by faith, which is the spiritual organ or faculty for receiving, appropriating, absorbing, or, if we may so speak, incorporating "spiritual meat" and "spiritual drink." So His life is infused and His Spirit is breathed, and His disposi-

tion of loyalty to God, devotion to righteousness, meekness and lowliness of heart are
formed in those that believe.

" Lord ! evermore give us this Bread !
  Thy flesh is meat indeed ; and Thy blood drink indeed !"

XXX.

DAY AND NIGHT.

"We must work the works of Him that sent me, while it is day: the night cometh, when no man can work."—St. John ix. 4.

To speak of life and death as day and night is so natural that one does not think of it as a metaphor. The illustration is among all authors and in all languages. It is also in common speech. Every man has his day. One has a longer day, another a shorter. One has a bright, another a shaded or even a stormy day. Then night falls, perhaps suddenly, as in the Tropics, where there is no twilight, and it is dark whenever the sun goes down; perhaps with a gentle and gradual descent, as in the far North or far South, where daylight lingers long and slowly fades away.

The metaphor easily lends itself to the frequent, and not always reasonable, complaints of the shortness of our earthly existence. Only a day! So our old poet Quarles wrote of life—

> " Whose glory in one day doth fill the stage
> With childhood, manhood, and decrepit age."

Jesus Christ, we may be sure, used the illustration in no querulous sense, but with a purpose worthy of His most genial and heavenly wisdom. He would impress on His disciples the value of time and opportunity, and admonish them to lay out their one and only day to good account. His own lifetime, and more especially the years allotted to His public career, formed His day. Abraham foresaw it, and was glad; though his degenerate offspring strove to make Christ's day bitter by their enmity, and even to cut it short by violence.* Now the Lord knew well that His would be a short and troubled day, but was content and tranquil through His perfect trust in the Heavenly Father, who had appointed to Him both His work and His time. No plot of the Jews could shorten His allotted day by one hour. It would

* St. John viii. 39, 40, 56.

end when the limit assigned to it by the
Father was reached, and when the work committed by the Father to the Son was accomplished.

Jesus had said to the Jews, that if they
were really Abraham's children, they would
".do the works of Abraham." Their conduct indicated rather that they were children
of the Devil. Then He taught the disciples
that He, as the Son of God, "must work
the works of God." And if the Revised Text
be correct in reading " we " instead of " I," He
invited the apostles to spend their day in the
same obedience.

The work of God which our Master was
about to perform was opening the eyes of
a man who had been born blind. In this we
may not be able to follow Him; but in the
general direction and use of life and its
opportunities, we may, we must. He is our
model, alike in the character of His occupa-
tions, which illustrated both the righteousness
and the mercy of God, and in the perseverance
with which, in the face of difficulty and " con-
tradiction of sinners," He continued His obedi-

ence till all was accomplished, and He could say to the Father, "I have glorified Thee on the earth; I have finished the work which Thou gavest Me to do." *

The first thought regarding life-work which presses upon men is this prosaic one, that they must work in order to live at all; must by some sort of exertion win their daily bread. Practically this is a universal law, and one that conduces to health and virtue. The exceptions to it are not so great or so many as a superficial observer may suppose; for there are many kinds of labour, and a thoroughly idle man is rare. Nor is the idler to be envied. He is usually discontented, and always trivial.

Jesus Christ did not claim exemption from the rule that man must work in order to subsist. There is no cause to doubt that in the years of His obscurity at Nazareth He wrought with His own hands, and so earned the plain bread of a carpenter's table. If afterwards, while labouring early and late in His prophetic office, He accepted the ministrations of others to His

* St. John xvii. 4.

necessity, or availed Himself of the hospitality of those who invited Him into their houses, He did what Eastern .prophets and teachers have always done, and discontinued manual work only that He might devote Himself without hindrance to that higher walk of duty which was appointed to Him by the Father. Thus our Saviour, in His humanity, knows the law of daily labour, and loves to see His followers industrious in their earthly callings and " diligent in business." On this, however, we need not dilate. Men are held to this by sheer necessity, or by the desire to accumulate property. There is more need to dwell on the obligations of the heavenly call- ing, and the diligence which Christians ought to show in working the works of God.

The first work is to believe on Him whom God has sent.* And this excludes at once all thought of working from and for ourselves in order to our justification and salvation. We are justified by faith ; we are saved by grace. "It is not of works, lest any man should boast." " Not by works of righteousness

* St. John vi. 28, 29.

which we have done, but according to His mercy God saved us." If anything is plainly taught in the New Testament, it is that no claim of human merit to the favour of God can be established. Our good works, if we venture so to call them, cannot obliterate or compensate for our misdeeds. At the best, they are faulty and imperfect, and can hardly answer for themselves. Divine grace is our only refuge. Yet this must not be turned into a bed of sloth, nor the denial of human merit made a pretence for neglecting or discouraging personal exertion. The Law said— Do and live! The Gospel says—Live and do! Grace does not dispense with doing, but, in order to it, supplies the motive and the strength.

He who is saved by grace is required to "work out his own salvation with fear and trembling." What the Spirit of God works in by the Word of truth the Christian is to work out in practice, *i.e.*, to develop and bring to manifestation and fruit-bearing. This, as every one knows who honestly tries it, is arduous work, and needs most close attention. It is the great task of self-discipline. It is to exercise the understanding, cultivate the conscience, and "above all keeping," keep the heart. It is to practise temperance in all things, striving for the mastery over passion and its various incitements. It is to "mortify our members which are upon the earth." It is to "give diligence to make our calling and election sure."

Moreover, there is the obligation to "do good to all men as we have opportunity, especially to those who are of the household of faith." This is the sort of work most obviously suggested by the language of our Lord; and, indeed, the care of our own spiritual life is apt to become morbid unless it is accompanied by unselfish exertion for the temporal and eternal benefit of others. Every child of God should delight in mercy. Every believer in Christ should walk in the steps of His unwearied beneficence.

For all there is but a day. Work while the day lasts! The time is long enough for glorifying God and finishing the work, if it be well employed, but too short to allow a margin for trifling. It is well when men begin early to attend to the things of the Heavenly Father, as Jesus did, and commence the Christian life in the morning of the natural life. It is well to do as Old Testament worthies did when they had a Divine errand to fulfil. They "gat up early in the morning."

Alas! some are no more than morning Christians. They promise well in childhood, but as their morning passes on to noon, they fall away. Their goodness is "like a morning cloud, and like the dew which quickly passes away." * Others postpone their religion till the evening. They trust to the sobering effect of age and the solemn thoughts which the decline of life suggests to all. They run a dreadful risk, for the night may come suddenly and cut off all their hopes; and even if they do find time to seek and serve God at last, it is a poor homage to Him to offer

* Hosea vi. 4.

the flagging energies and very dregs of life. Evening is no time for beginning the Christian course. Men ought to devote their whole life-day to learning the will of God and doing His works.

"The night cometh, when no man can work." This statement does not hold good of night in our Western countries, where so many toil by artificial light all through the night in iron and steel works, where the furnaces are never allowed to cool; in mines, where there is a "night-shift;" in printing-offices, and on railways. But in Palestine and throughout Syria the rule is absolute that work ceases when the sun goes down. It is not the custom to go abroad at night even for amusement, and work is not attempted. The poor, dim lamplight is of itself sufficient to forbid night labour. So the contrast is maintained which was expressed by one of the old Hebrew bards. The beasts of the forest prowl forth at night, and at sunrise "lay themselves down in their dens." Man, on the contrary, begins his activity in the morning. He "goes forth unto his work and labour until the evening." *

Some have thought it scarcely worthy of the Lord to describe the end of a good and obedient life as dark and silent night. Such language has appeared to them to savour of Old Testament dimness, or even of heathen gloom, concerning the future state. But it should be observed that night is here described as following day in order that rest may follow toil. In this view it is not black or appalling. It is welcome to those who have spent a long and busy day. How beautiful is night! How good it is when "He gives His beloved sleep!"

It is not eternal sleep. The night endures only till the day of glory breaks from heaven. O happy morning when the Lord shall appear and the sleeping saints shall rise to meet Him —none of them old or feeble, but all in fresh vigour for the service of their God and King! Then shall they go forth again to work the works of God; but we must not say "till the

* Ps. civ. 20-23.

evening." There is no end to that life ; there is no night in heaven.

> " Pray that when thy life is closing,
>   Calm reposing,
>   Thou mayst die, and not in pain ;
>   That, the night of death departed,
>   Thou, glad-hearted,
>   Mayst behold the Sun again." *

---

* Von Canitz in Lyra Germanica.

XXXI.

THE DOOR AND THE SHEPHERD.

" I am the door: by Me if any man enter in, he shall be saved, and shall go in and go out, and shall find pasture. . . . I am the Good Shepherd: the good shepherd layeth down his life for the sheep."—St. John x. 9, 11.

Is this an instance of mixed metaphor? Not so much so as may appear to those who do not know or bear in mind the pastoral usages of the East. Sheepfolds there are open spaces surrounded by solid stone walls. They are for the protection of flocks from robbers and from beasts of prey, and have but one narrow gate for entrance and for exit. The shepherd is not a servant hired for wages, but the owner of the sheep, and, as a matter of course, has the right of entrance into the fold by the gate or door. If he has a man in charge as porter, at his approach the porter opens. Thieves and robbers have to climb over the wall.

Indeed, the shepherd may himself be called the door. He stands there as the sheep pass in or pass out, examines them one by one to see that none has been hurt, and counts them to make sure that not one has been lost. It is at his bidding that they seek the fold for shelter. He goes before and leads them thither. Again, it is at his bidding that they go out to find pasture; and when he has passed them through the gate, he shows them the way, and they follow his steps. The shepherd leads them in and out.

As between the Arab and his horse, so also between the Syrian shepherd and his sheep the relation is very intimate. They have a perfect mutual understanding. They spend long hours together in solitary places, share the same dangers, and are companions both in storm and in sunshine. The shepherd " cares for the sheep," knows one from another by minute marks unnoticed by a stranger, and calls them individually by name. The sheep in turn recognise their human friend and guardian, grow familiar with his voice, come at his call, tread in his steps. So the

sheep, by their attachment to him, are kept
from straying into danger, while he, on his
part, keeps a vigilant eye upon them, and is
ready at a moment to rescue any one of them
from danger.   A shepherd in Palestine is
always armed, and will use his weapon rather
than let any beast of prey, or any robber,
pluck a sheep out of his care.

How dear to Christ are His redeemed
people—His own sheep! How dear should
Christ be to them!

The illustration comes down from the Old
Testament, in which appeal is made to
Jehovah as the Shepherd of Israel, who had
led His people as a flock "by the hand of
Moses and Aaron." *   The rulers in the Theo-
cracy were official shepherds under Jehovah,
and when they were unfaithful to their trust,
they were sharply censured in the Scriptures
of the Prophets.†   At the time when Christ
appeared, the under-shepherds of the chosen
people had quite lost the true pastoral affection, and were oppressing and scattering the
flock.   Then He proclaimed a new mission

* Ps. lxxx. 1.   † See Jer. xxiii.; Ezek. xxxiv.

from God to the "lost sheep of the house of Israel." And other sheep He had given to Him from among the Gentiles, whom He would gather into the one flock of God.

The saying, "I am the Good Shepherd," is one of those phrases of self-assertion which are so significant as proceeding from the lips of the meek and lowly Jesus. It is in the same category with "I am the Light of the World;" "I am the Bread of Life;" "I am the True Vine,"—phrases all of them which let him pronounce exaggerated who dare, but which we must regard as the expression of a conscious relation to the life of all mankind, and of a sublime power to save.

St. Peter, who had himself been specially charged to feed the sheep and lambs of Christ, writes of his Master as "the Chief Shepherd." The author of the Epistle to the Hebrews calls Him "that great Shepherd of the sheep." The rough drawings found in the Roman Catacombs show how dear the thought of this Heavenly Shepherd was to the early Christians in their days of trial.

The epithet "good" refers not so much

to benevolence as to His being the genuine Shepherd, in contrast with hirelings who cared not for the sheep. And the proofs of this are two :—

I. *His intimacy with the flock.*

" I know My sheep, and am known of Mine." He is the Door through which they pass in and out, or the Shepherd at the door taking cognisance of every one. And He is their Keeper in the open field—taking notice of this one as it feeds, and that one as it rests beside the still waters, and that other as it thoughtlessly strays towards the thicket where some ravenous beast may lurk. He calls each by name.

In turn, the sheep know Him, and therefore trust, obey, and follow Him. Whatever Christians are ignorant of, they know Christ. His love constrains them; His care encompasses them on every side so that, whether quietly folded, or out on the hillside exposed to dangers, they are safe with Him. And this is a knowledge which grows with every day of Christian experience. The Lord's people may discern fresh proofs of His presence and pastoral care every day and almost every hour, in checks and reverses as well as in encouragements and successes, in supply of wants, relief of apprehensions, help for infirmities, in the signs of an unwearied patience and unfailing sympathy.

No object in heaven or earth can induce this Shepherd to forget His flock. No teacher or guide can induce the flock to desert this Shepherd. A stranger they will not follow.

II. *His surrender of His own life for the sheep.*

A wolf or a robber would destroy; a hireling would flee to secure his own safety, leaving the flock to be ravaged; but the Good Shepherd was ready to lay down His own life that His sheep might not perish.

With a glorious resignation Jesus saw the approach of death. The fearful Cross was already throwing its shadow on His path; and although the sacrificial character and purport of His decease at Jerusalem could not yet be openly declared to others, to His own mind all was clear. He was to be slain by the wicked and unjust hands of cruel men; but in submitting to this, He would accomplish the redemption of His flock. To God the Father Almighty He would surrender His life and pour out His soul, an offering and a sacrifice. In Him was to be fulfilled the ancient oracle, "Awake, O sword, against My Shepherd, against the Man that is My fellow (nearest one)."* The sword of the Lord was to pierce Him for the transgressions of His people to be gathered out of all nations; and by the laying down of His life they are ransomed.

He had power to lay down His life, and power to take it again. In His retaken or resurrection life He is now watching over His flock as "the Shepherd and Bishop of souls." It is He who increases the flock by going after lost sheep in the power of the Spirit with the word of the Gospel, and brings back penitents one by one. It is He who tends and nourishes the young and inex-

* Zech. xiii. 7.

perienced, for "He gathers lambs with His arm, and carries them in His bosom." Never sinner returned to God but was recovered by this Good Shepherd; never a young beginner in the faith grew to maturity but under the patient and loving care of Jesus. It is He who folds His flock in the temporary shelter appointed for the Church on earth. If any one who has erred and strayed as a lost sheep, but has repented, be afraid or ashamed to join himself to the people of God, let him be encouraged by the double metaphor which is the theme of our present study, and lay it to heart that this Shepherd Himself is the Door. He gives admission to whomsoever He will. He will not merely let in, but carry in on His shoulder a lost sheep that He has found. And whom Christ admits, who has authority to exclude? No doubt there is a porter at the gate, a useful servant. Let this represent Church regulation and discipline, highly useful in its place for the protection of the fold from the inroad of the ungodly and the profane. But this is right only as it is directed by the mind of Christ, and subordinated to His word. The porter must obey the Shepherd's voice, and must open the gate without question at His approach. When the Lord passes in or carries in a lost sheep that He has found, the porter has nothing to do but stand by and rejoice.

The Lord has but one flock, gathered from north, south, east, and west. In this world, however, they are not put into one fold. Every one knows that the expression to that effect in the Authorised Version of St. John's Gospel is a sheer mistranslation. It has done much harm in its time. "One fold" has been the watchword of those who have insisted on conformity to one visible Church, with definite limits, uniform institutions, and universal authority. But the watchword is nothing more than an incorrect rendering, and the assumption based upon it is a fallacy. It ignores a great distinction between the Israel of God and the Church of God. The unity of Israel was that of one fold as well as one flock. Around the chosen nation was a stone wall of "commandments contained in ordinances," and an enforced separation from other nations. But the Church is one flock with many folds. To attempt to build a uniform stone wall about it is to mistake the nature of our dispensation, and to environ the freemen of Christ with an intolerable tyranny. The one flock, or Church catholic, existed at the beginning, and exists now, in " the Churches" which are folded here or there as is most convenient, and not always or everywhere in folds of the same shape or size, but with diversities for which there is scope enough without any real disturbance of Church unity.

A well-instructed Christian will set a just value on the fold, but will not exaggerate its importance. He will not give countenance to separatists, who find fault with all established order, and love to draw away a few sheep into some self-chosen nook, where they complacently regard themselves as the saints, the holy brethren, the faithful few. But, on the other hand, he will never disown fellow-Christians on the ground that they are not within the same fold with himself. A certain amount of form is good, but no form is indispensable or vital. Let the best form of fold be learned from the New Testament and from Christian history, and let existing forms .be respected in so far as they agree with the ideal best. But form, after all, is only form; and there is no harm in variety so long as truth is guarded, life cherished, and charity increased.

Whatever the style of fold, that man is received into the Church of God who is admitted by the Chief Shepherd. He is the Door. And whosoever in any place is growing in Christian knowledge, love, and steadfastness, gives evidence that he is living under the same Chief Shepherd's gracious care. No ecclesiastical theory can be true which would force us to dispute such propositions as these. If any man love God and follow after righteousness, it is because the Good Shepherd has taught him so to do. If any man be nourished in good doctrine, cheered by Divine promises, kept in hours of temptation, delivered from the bondage of evil habit, whatever be the mediate influences or ministrations employed, the ultimate reason is that he has been so nourished, comforted, preserved, and delivered by Him whose "own the sheep are," and who has revealed His purpose regarding them in these memorable words, "I give unto them eternal life; and they shall never perish, and no one shall snatch them out of My hand."

XXXII.

A GRAIN OF WHEAT.

"Verily, verily, I say unto you, Except a grain of wheat fall into the earth and die, it abideth by itself alone; but if it die, it beareth much fruit. He that loveth his life loseth it; and he that hateth his life in this world shall keep it unto life eternal."—St. John xii. 24, 25.

It was a significant circumstance that, when the Jews were hastening to a final rejection of the Messiah, certain Greeks desired that they might "see Him." The time of exclusive ministry to "the lost sheep of the house of Israel" was drawing to a close, and the era of grace to all nations was at hand. Of this there is distinct indication in the language of Jesus to the two disciples who conveyed to Him the request of the Greeks, probably in the hearing of those anxious or curious inquirers. He spoke of Himself as the Son of Man, as though to emphasise His kinship in humanity to the Gentiles as well as to the Jews. And He intimated the approach of a time when He would cast an attractive power over all nations. Not only might He be seen by a few Greeks, who probably were proselytes of the gate, having come up to Jerusalem for the Feast of the Passover; He would be proclaimed in the gospel "to every creature," without distinction of nation or locality. He would draw all to Himself.

But before this could be, Jesus Christ must needs suffer and die. An unwelcome truth this to the disciples, and a perplexing one, no doubt, to the inquiring Greeks; but a condition of His success which profoundly impressed the soul of Jesus, and carried with it a far-reaching lesson for His Church in all ages. He was to be lifted up on the Cross in order to draw. He was to suffer that He might enter into His glory.

The occasion accounts for the terms in which our Lord foretold His death and its results. There was no reference to its sacrificial import, as there might have been if He had been speaking exclusively to Jews or Galileans familiar with the Old Testament propitiatory system. There was no statement of the Godward aspect and efficacy of His death as an atonement for sin. The view of "His decease at Jerusalem" which the occasion suggested and called forth was that it would constitute Him a Saviour for all the nations, and so glorify Him upon the earth.

For the elucidation of this view the grain of wheat was a happy illustration. While simple and easily remembered, it set forth in a most instructive manner the great fact and natural law of death and resurrection in order to fruitfulness. The metaphor recurs in St. Paul's famous passage on the resurrection of "the dead in Christ." "That which thou sowest is not quickened except it die." *

Look at a grain of wheat as it may lie in your hand or on the hard surface of the ground. It is a thing of life, but cannot show or propagate its life or bring forth any fruit. For all that it yields, it might as well be a little stone or a rough grain of yellow gravel. It abides alone. Now this is what Jesus Christ would not consent to be. True that He was alone in His suffering for our sin.

* 1 Cor. xv. 36–38, 43, 44.

Even His three chosen disciples could not watch with Him one hour so as to help Him by their sympathy. The Father was with Him; but on the Cross He was absolutely alone, as indicated by the pathetic cry, " My God, my God! why hast Thou forsaken Me?" All this, however, He endured that He might not be alone in the ages to come. In "justifying many" He would "see of the travail of His soul and be satisfied." * He would not save Himself just that He might save others. The Shepherd would gather a flock. The Bridegroom would redeem and win a bride. "It is not good that the man should be alone." The Prince of Life, rising again out of death, would give life to the world, and all His followers would be sharers of His own fruit-bearing life, and so ultimately of His heavenly rest and glory.

But as the grain of wheat, if not sown in the earth, abides alone, so Jesus Christ would have failed of His great purpose if He had not died. No doubt His personal character and history would have made a certain im-

* Isaiah liii. 11.

pression, and His teaching might have transmitted His name to future generations as that of the most profound and spiritual of all the Jewish Rabbis; but from Him could have proceeded no vitalising power. There would have been neither redemption nor regeneration of men. If Jesus had not endured the Cross, or if, after He was nailed upon it and lifted up from the earth, He had "come down from the Cross" at the challenge of the mocking bystanders, He would never have been a Redeemer or a Prince of Life to others. He would not have taken even one of the children of men to Paradise. He would have continued alone.

Take the grain of wheat to the ploughed field, and sow or hide it in the earth. There ensues a marvellous change. The berry * dissolves or dies, and lo! a plant of wheat striking root in the soil and sending up a green

* "The original word is not *sperma*, a seed, but *kokkos*, a berry, a fruit. It shows the extreme, even scientific, accuracy of our Saviour's language; for the corn of wheat, and other cereal grains, consist of seeds incorporated with seed-vessels, and are in reality fruits, although they appear like seeds. It is not the bare seed that falls into the ground, and, by dying, yields much fruit, but the corn of wheat—the whole fruit with its husk-like coverings."—*MacMillan's* "*True Vine*," p. 166, 3d edit.

blade above the surface, which becomes a strong stalk and bears a head of corn. The wheat which was found in the hand of an Egyptian mummy had not lost its reproductive power through all the long ages while it continued shut up and " alone." So soon as it was sown in the earth, it died and lived again, bringing forth much fruit. One grain of wheat passing through this process produces many grains. So Jesus Christ, through death and resurrection, was to yield fruit abundantly.

The rationale of the vegetable reproduction no one can fully explain. Little wonder, then, that the spiritual transformation which it is here taken to illustrate should baffle our analysis. But the fact is beyond doubt to any one who believes the sayings of Christ. By dying and rising again He gives life to the world. He does not, He cannot, " continue alone." Every day His fruit is on the increase. And as we see the attractive power of the Saviour over all nations, new disciples gained, new trophies of salvation won, new congregations gathered, new missions opened, the name of Jesus growing greater and His influence more extensive in all regions of the earth, what can we think of it all but that " the corn of wheat " that died at Jerusalem is bringing forth much fruit?

We have said that the condition of our Lord's success here illustrated conveys a far-reaching lesson to His Church. Jesus did not leave this to be inferred. He taught it explicitly. The case of the Son of Man was to be the supreme instance, but far from the only instance, of a great principle or law of success. Men are saved not merely by the grace of Christ, but in and through a process of conformity to Him. They, after His example, make a self-surrender and self-oblation in order to a higher life and fruitfulness.

Before our Lord went up to Jerusalem to suffer, He said some weighty words to this effect in the hearing of a great multitude, who followed Him with a very inadequate conception of what might be involved in adherence to Him and to His gospel. " If any man come unto Me, and hate not his own father, and mother, and wife, and children, and brethren, and sisters, yea, and his own life also, he cannot be My disciple. Whosoever doth not bear his own cross, and come after Me, cannot be My disciple." * Through this severe ordeal, in a very literal sense, the apostles and primitive Christians had to pass, surrendering intimacies, forfeiting friendships, conferring not with flesh and blood of their nearest kindred, enduring reproach from their neighbours, "taking joyfully the spoiling of their goods," and putting life itself in peril for their Divine Master's name. Many even of those who were favourably disposed towards Him must have shrunk from such an abandonment of all for His sake. They could not be His disciples.

But to hate one's own life! Is this possible? And, if possible, is it right? Our Lord evidently used the phrase in the sense of not clinging to life or counting it dear. And at Jerusalem He returned to the point with one of those paradoxical terms of expression which He sometimes employed the better to drive home His teachings. "He that loveth his life loseth it, and he that hateth his life in this world shall keep it unto life eternal." That it is both possible and right to subordinate the love of life to great and worthy objects surely needs no argument. Both

* St. Luke xiv. 26, 27.

heathens and Christians judge that patriots have done well to die for their country. Men stationed at critical posts of duty, on whose continuance there many lives have depended in some hour of danger, have done well to die at their posts. In like manner the martyrs have done well who dared to die rather than repudiate or dishonour Christ. Long before St. Paul finished his course by martyrdom he died daily. Far from loving his own life, he poured it out without stint in the service of Christ and the Church. He was almost too " ready to die at Jerusalem for the name of the Lord Jesus;" and he wrote with a fine glow of feeling to his much-cherished brethren at Philippi, " Yea, and if I am offered upon the sacrifice (poured out as a drink-offering) and service of your faith, I joy and rejoice with you all." [*] There were many of the same self-devoting spirit, *e.g.*, Epaphroditus, "who for the work of Christ came nigh unto death, hazarding his life." [†]

It is proper to note that when our Lord spoke of a life to be loved or hated, and of a life eternal to be gained, He used two quite

* Phil. ii. 17.　　　† Phil. ii. 30.

distinct words. The former, which is rendered "the soul" in the margin of the Revised Version, is the $\psi v \chi \eta$; the latter is $\zeta \omega \eta$. The former is that life of sensation and natural desire which sickness weakens and death terminates. It feels at home in the "psychical body," and seeking satisfaction largely through the body, shrinks from loss and pain and all that threatens its dissolution. Of this the Lord said that if a man cares more for the mortal life and its enjoyments than for Him, he cannot be His disciple. And, far from speaking as many religious people nowadays do, of the love of souls, Jesus Christ said that if a man egotistically loves and pets his own soul, he loses it. He overreaches himself. Not using life unselfishly for Christ and the promotion of mercy and truth, he makes nothing of it but failure. He may seem to prosper, and may have length of days; but the issue is—a lost soul.

On the other hand, whosoever holds this present life with its desires and capacities in subordination to Christ and the kingdom of heaven, and aims at serving and glorifying

God at whatsoever cost or risk, shall keep the life which he seems to hate unto life everlasting. This is the ζωη—the same word as in the phrases, " in Him was life," " the crown of life," " the bread of life," " life and godliness." This is that life of union with the risen Prince of Life into which they are admitted, and in which they are kept, who spend, and if need be sacrifice, their life in this world for His sake and the gospel's.

Thus both the example and the teaching of Christ condemn the self-seeking and self-sparing which are, alas! so common among those who wear the Christian name. If we be His disciples, we must give up something of our ease in order to have a better consolation. We must lose in order to win, and die in order to live. If we preserve ourselves too carefully, we prove fruitless, and " abide alone." But if we devote ourselves in love to the service of Jesus Christ and of mankind, we live and fructify.

We have seen that the growth of the Church is due to the grain of wheat that died in the ground and sprung up again at

Jerusalem, *i.e.*, to the death and resurrection of Jesus Christ. If any ask why the Church does not grow more rapidly, we believe that this is due mainly to the failure of so many Christians to obey the word and follow the example of their Heavenly Master. In ever so many quarters where Christ is preached and Church ordinances are regularly observed, there seems to be little fruit. A dull average is maintained. When you revisit such places, perhaps after a lapse of years, you find no enlargement or expansion. All things continue as they were. Why is this? Is the gospel stricken with palsy? Is the Spirit of the Lord straitened? Nay; but the Christianity current there is of a formal, lukewarm type, which produces no effect and exerts no attractive influence. There is no self-denial or self-devotion to Christ and His cause on the part of those who profess to believe the gospel and ought to have received the Spirit. The wheat lies in a sack idle and unproductive. What is wanted all round for the increase of the Church is a more complete devotion of the followers of Christ to a service that should be dearer to them than life itself.

We have never seen a man thus devoted and yet destitute of fruit; but we have seen many who had splendid opportunities of usefulness pass their years to very little purpose, simply because they had never learned the secret of losing in order to gain, and denying themselves in order to prevail. The visible Church, even in its purest and best branches, is weakened and hindered by its own half-hearted ministers and members, who live at ease and know nothing of taking up every man his own cross or following the Son of Man in an obedience which will not spare or humour the flesh. These cannot be His disciples. But the reproach of barrenness would soon be rolled away if even a good proportion of those who look to Jesus Christ for pardon would follow Him in service. "Dying, and behold we live;" * and living in the power of the Spirit, we bring forth much fruit.

* 2 Cor. vi. 9.

XXXIII.

THE BATH AND THE BASON.

" Jesus saith to him, He that is bathed needeth not save to wash his feet, but is clean every whit : and ye are clean, but not all."—St. John xiii. 10.

In a bath, the whole body is plunged and purified; in a bason, one part of the body, as the hands or feet. An Eastern who bathes before a banquet may need the bason to cleanse his feet from dust that they may have gathered on the way from the bathroom to the guest-chamber; or, taking ever so short a walk in sandals, he must have water poured over his feet, and a servant with bason and towel to wait upon him before he sits down to meat. With His wonted felicity of illustration, our Lord used this familiar custom to inculcate moral and spiritual truth.

This language recalls Old Testament symbolism. Not that our Saviour made such reference, for He was not discussing any question of religious worship, but teaching a lesson of brotherly love; but it suggests itself. Before Aaron and his sons were invested with the robes of priesthood, Moses had it in command from God that they should bathe in water; and then, after they had bathed and donned their robes, they needed before each act of service to wash their hands and feet at the laver in the court of the tabernacle. Every year thereafter, on that day of atonement which raised the priesthood in Israel to its highest point of privilege in the entrance of the high priest as intercessor into the holy of holies, that impersonation of all Israel was required to bathe, and wash his flesh in water, before he put on his linen garments of office.

The law of "divers washings" has passed away with those of "meats and drinks and carnal ordinances." The High Priest of our profession is the undefiled Jesus, who, having entered into the holiest, abides there, making continual intercession for us. We also serve as priests unto God; but we may not do so without a moral and spiritual purification. This we have obtained as having once bathed and being "once purged." And this we must have renewed in order to the continu-. ance of our service. Because we are so apt to be soiled in the world, and even to sin amidst holy duties, we have need of the bason after the bath. Though we are clean, we need to wash our hands and our feet.

But this, as we have pointed out, was not our Saviour's theme in the supper-chamber at Jerusalem. He was indicating not the conditions of Christian worship, but the right temper and spirit for Christian intercourse and the Christian walk. He pronounced all the apostles to be clean, all but one, on whom the Master's cleansing word had not produced its due effect—Judas the traitor. The eleven had passed through the bath. Therefore Simon Peter was mistaken in asking the Lord to pour water over his head and body, as though he were still among the uncleansed. His impulsive request showed a want of spiritual intelligence, a defective appreciation of what Jesus had already done for him and his colleagues in separating them from the mass of their countrymen and making them clean through His word.

We have seen the same mistake among Christian people who have been ill taught or have not understood good teaching. They put themselves among the unconverted and unpardoned, supposing this to be the dictate of humility. They pray to be brought to the knowledge of the truth. They are always proposing to begin to be Christians. So they are of little service to Christ or His Church, because they are not sure that they are His disciples. They cannot tell whether He has cleansed them by His Word. It is difficult to do them any spiritual good. The bason is for those only who have been in the bath; therefore the question of the bath should first be decided. To have bathed does not imply that we are perfect, but means that we are separated from the unholy and profane, by the blood of Christ purging our consciences and the Word of Christ in the Spirit purifying our hearts.

He who is a stranger to grace and to God

needs the bath before all. He who has bathed still needs the bason, because it is only too easy for him to compromise his integrity and defile himself again with stains of sin and dust of worldliness.* If he has a tender conscience, he cannot bear to wait on the Lord or sup with the Lord with soiled feet; so he calls for the bason. "Wash me, and I shall be whiter than snow." And the Holy Saviour, on His part, cannot bear to have His servants tarnished with sin of daily life. However small the stains, He detects them; and He must wash the feet of His servants, or else disown them and say that they have no part with Him.

The Lord used this metaphor not so much with reference to the pardon of sin and purging of conscience from guilt as to set forth the cleansing of the mind and heart from worldliness and fleshly desire, in order to a continual fitness for Christian fellowship and service. And it is He who bestows both the initial blessing of the bath and the continued

* "Quis enim in hâc vita sic mundus, ut non sit magis magisque mundandus?"—*August. in Joann.* xv. 2.

blessing of the bason.   It was He who made the disciples " clean through His word ; " and it was He who washed their feet.   We also may, as His servants, do something to put sinful men into the bath, if only by urging on their consciences the Lord's command, " Wash ye, make you clean." *   And we are bound by His example and precept to take the bason and " wash the saints' feet."   It is a good piece of Christian service to remove the dust from some pilgrim who is weary and perhaps distressed, and, with unaffected acts of kindness and words of cleansing power uttered in the Spirit, refresh his heart, renew his heavenward purpose, and fit him for a closer and a purer walk with God.   If we know these things, happy are we if we do them.

* Isaiah i. 16–18.

XXXIV.

THE TRUE VINE.

"I am the true vine, and My Father is the husbandman. Every branch in Me that beareth not fruit, He taketh it away: and every branch that beareth fruit, He cleanseth it, that it may bear more fruit. Already ye are clean because of the word which I have spoken unto you. Abide in Me, and I in you. As the branch cannot bear fruit of itself, except it abide in the vine; so neither can ye, except ye abide in Me. I am the vine, ye are the branches: he that abideth in Me, and I in him, the same beareth much fruit: for apart from Me ye can do nothing."—St. John xv. 1–5.

A living writer who has given us a careful monogram on this theme, observes that "the vine, take it all in all, is the most perfect of plants. Some plants possess one part or one quality more highly developed; but for the harmonious development of every part and quality, for perfect balance of loveliness and usefulness, there is none to equal the vine. It belongs to the highest order of the vegetable kingdom, ranks in structure above the lily and the palm, occupies the same position among plants which man does among animals. Its stem and leaves are among the most elegant in shape and hue, its blossoms among the most modest and fragrant, while its fruit is botanically the most perfect." *

The higher grounds of Judea possess the very soil and climate that suit this noble plant. Even now, after long centuries of neglect and desolation, the eye is pleased with the sight of vineyards on the hills of Judah; and in ancient times these formed a great element in the beauty and prosperity of the Holy Land. After coming from Egypt and passing through Northern Arabia, the Israelites were amazed at the clusters of grapes brought by the scouts from the neighbourhood of Hebron. In after-times a happy peasantry occupied the land, every man resting under his own vine and his own fig-tree.

A natural object so valuable and so familiar was sure to find a place in religious symbolism. So we meet with it often in the Old Testament applied to uses of correction and instruc-

---

* The True Vine, by Dr. H. MacMillan, 3d edit., p. 32.

tion in righteousness; and it occurs in no fewer than five of our Lord's parables. The reference which He made to it on the night in which He was betrayed, if less than a parable, is more than the term metaphor can express. It is a kind of allegory, and was doubtless suggested by incidents of the hour. At the Last Supper Jesus had spoken of "the fruit of the vine." After supper He held a memorable conversation on life and grace, replying to observations and questions of the apostles Peter, Thomas, Philip, and Jude, and ending with the words, "Arise, let us go hence." Then the disciples, we may be sure, rose from table and formed a group around Him, hanging on His lips; and we know that He continued to speak to the eleven, and then poured out His heart in prayer to the Father before He proceeded to the garden at the foot of the Mount of Olives. It is not necessary to suppose that He pointed to an actual vine climbing up the wall of the house and twining about a verandah or the lattice of the upper chamber, though there is nothing forced or unlikely in such a conjecture. The position in which He stood when He rose from the supper couch, with the disciples surrounding Him, was of itself sufficient to suggest a vine with its many branches centring in one stem and root.

There could be no uncertainty as to His meaning. There are many clinging plants which may be called vines, as the bryony, the Virginian creeper, and the strawberry, but there is one grape vine. There was a vine of Sodom, the colocynth, bearing poisonous fruit; but apples of Sodom are not grapes.

The Lord called Himself "the True Vine." It is not the true as opposed to false, but the genuine and perfect as distinguished from the shadowy, imperfect, and inadequate.* Manna in the wilderness had been a daily bread, but it was not "the true bread from heaven." † Israel had been a vine brought by the Lord out of Egypt, a country unsuited to its life, and planted in the land of Canaan; but it was not the true vine. All the pains taken

---

* On the difference between ἀληθής, ἀληθινός, see Trench's New Testament Synonyms.

† St. John vi. 32.

with it did not prevent its degeneracy. And Jehovah uttered this reproach through his servant Jeremiah, "I had planted thee a noble vine, wholly a right seed : how then art thou turned into the degenerate plant of a strange vine unto Me?" * What was faultily and inadequately exhibited in Israel is fulfilled in Jesus Christ. Israel was the Lord's servant to show forth His praise among the nations, but proved unfaithful and unprofitable. Jesus Christ came as the Lord's Elect Servant, and did always the things that pleased the Father. In like manner Israel was the plant that became a degenerate or wild vine, and Jesus Christ was the True Vine, ever alive and fruitful to God. In Judah of old was the vine, and Benjamin was "the man of the right hand;" but Jesus Christ was the True Vine of Judah, and the Benjamin, the Son of Man who is "the Man of God's right hand." †

The vine has a very vigorous life; but for its development and fertility it is very de-

* Jer. ii. 21.   See also Isa. v. 1–7 ; Hosea x. 1.
† See Ps. lxxx. 14–17.

pendent on careful cultivation. It needs the watchful eye and deft hand of a vine-dresser. And this is not wanting to the True Vine. Jesus said, " My Father is the husband- man." The word employed denotes not a hired labourer, but the owner of the vine, who puts his own hand to the work of train- ing and pruning it.*

Although much was made of this expression of our Lord by the Arians, it can hardly be necessary now to point out that Christ's sub- ordination to and dependence on the Father during His mission to this world in no wise contradicts the doctrine of the oneness of the Father and the Son in the Blessed Trinity. It is one thing to state the doctrine of revela- tion regarding the essential Divine existence, which is unity in trinity ; it is another thing altogether to describe the Divine method of human salvation in which the Son is subor- dinated to the Father, and the Holy Spirit to the Father and the Son. Many sound theo- logians have explained this subordination (as

* It is the term applied in the Septuagint version of Gen. ix. 20 to Noah, and in 2 Chron. xxvi. 10 to King Uzziah.

in the expression "My Father is greater than I") by the humanity of our Saviour. But this is not satisfactory. There was no need to state that God the Father Almighty was greater than Jesus, considered simply as a man. The position of the servant, the messenger, the inferior, was that which not merely the Man, but the God-Man accepted while He passed through His "state of humiliation" in order to be our Prince and Saviour.

As the vine belongs to the husbandman, so "Christ is God's." * As the branches belong to the vine, and so to the husbandman, Christians are Christ's, and so in the possession and the care of God.

Our Saviour, being intent on lifting the thoughts of His disciples to the Father, taught them that the Father had planted the True Vine in the earth in the gift and incarnation of the Son, and that He would care for and lovingly tend that Vine and all its branches. The supports of grace and the pruning-strokes of discipline are all of Him.

Under the eye and hand of an owner who

* 1 Cor. iii. 23.

looks after it himself, a vine will send forth branches and tendrils on every side, filled with its own strong vitality. So under the grace and providence of the Heavenly Father, Jesus Christ was to produce, and is still producing, disciples on every side, who are not merely instructed in His doctrine, but also imbued with His Spirit. Indeed this figure of a vine and its branches is perhaps the best of all the Biblical illustrations of the intimate union between Christ and His disciples. That of the shepherd and the sheep gives us the thought of intimacy, but it is between a guardian who is of a superior order and creatures of an inferior grade whom he watches over and protects. That of a husband and wife gives the ideas of intimacy and union, and between two beings of the same order; but they are two persons with independent lives, and one of them lives on though the other has died. That of the head and members, so much used by St. Paul, illustrates one life common to the whole body, but it falls short in not being able to express the constant putting forth of new growths. A human body has but a limited and fixed number of members, whereas a vine year by year shoots forth new twigs and branches.

Each new branch is itself a fresh young vine growing on the wood formed by the branches which are its ancestors. So every living Christian is added to the Church, and is himself a small vine growing out of the original Vine, which is Christ, and all the Christians of past times who are not dead but alive in Him.

A vine lives in its branches, and draws in nourishment and animation through its leaves. A vine without branches would be a mere stick, dry and useless, and would never answer for an emblem of Jesus Christ, who would not " abide alone," but surrounded Himself with disciples, and provided for the transmission and propagation of His living effluence through them. On the other hand, branches want the support of the vine stem, and the life impelled from the root. As Christ would be incomplete and " alone " without Christians, so Christians would be nothing without Him. Apart from Him they can do nothing.

As every one knows, the vine is cultivated solely for its fruit. It has luxuriant foliage and graceful tendrils, but it would not pay for the labour expended on it if it did not yield grapes. This is a point strongly urged in condemnation of the people of Jerusalem by the pen of the prophet Ezekiel.* The wood is fit for nothing but fuel; and so the vine of Judah yielding no fruit to Jehovah, was in danger of burning judgment. Accordingly the disciples were instructed that the True Vine existed and was tended by the Heavenly Father entirely with a view to fruit on the branches—the "fruit of righteousness, which is by Jesus Christ to the glory and praise of God." It was, so to speak, the very object which the True Vine had in view in producing and sustaining its branches. "I chose you and appointed you, that ye should go and bear fruit." † It is also the wish of the Husbandman, and is the only proper return or response that can be made to His watchful care. "Herein is My Father glorified, that ye bear much fruit." ‡

* Chap. xv.　　　† Ver. 16.　　　‡ Ver. 8.

It has been said too absolutely that "it is fruit that Christ wants, not works." He wants works from those who believe on His name, as we learn in express terms both from Him and His apostles.* But in some respects the word fruit certainly gives a better conception of what Christian obedience should be. Works may be performed from a variety of motives, but fruit must be the spontaneous product of an inward disposition. Works may be done by a combination of Christians in a Church or society, in which it is difficult to assign to each person his share, but fruit comes out in distinct individual detail. The vinedresser can see what each branch or twig bears, and can cut off the fruitless and therefore superfluous wood. So the Father in heaven takes cognisance of the individual fruit-bearing of every one who professes to be Christ's; and in all His care of the vine, even in His sharpest pruning, He aims at an increase of the fruit of righteousness.

Grapes from ordinary vines are easily blighted, and, at their best, if not gathered

* St. John ix. 4, xiv. 12 ; Eph. ii. 10 ; James ii. 26.

for food or for wine-making, they fall to the earth and perish; but it was the pleasure of Him who is the True Vine to produce through the disciples, who were His branches, fruit that "should abide."* Efforts of men in their own strength, ever so well meant, how little comes of them! The paths of history are strewn with withered blossoms, abortive buds, and perishing fruit. Early promise of goodness without life in Christ, how it passes away and is forgotten! In mid-life there is blight, and in old age barrenness and vanity. But Jesus Christ, in and through His disciples, yields permanent results in their lives to His Father's glory. He causes them to continue in His commandments, and so also in His love. He holds them in vital union with Himself, as branches abiding in the Vine; and then, by His Word abiding in them and the Spirit of His life flowing into them, He forms and matures them to a consistence of character which has precious and enduring fruit. Thus His joy continues to be in them, and their joy in Him is fulfilled. They have

* Ver. 16.

" fruit unto holiness, and the end everlasting life." *

How true this has been of those first branches, the band of disciples to whom Christ spoke this allegory! Of other men who lived at that period, and whose names rang through the Roman world, what remains? Names have come down to us, and a few books and laws, because these appeal to intellect and the sense of justice; but of all that men did or accumulated for their own ends, we find nothing but a few ruins. Contrast with this the case of those men of Galilee whom Jesus Christ sent forth in His name and with His Spirit to yield fruit to God in preaching peace and doing good to men. What grand results from them! Their fruit remains to this day. Theirs, and the fruit of those who have followed their faith, and drawn from the same Vine-root of perpetual life, is precious and fragrant in many lands, giving glory to Jesus and to His Father in heaven.

* Romans vi. 22.

XXXV.

TRAVAIL.

"A woman when she is in travail hath sorrow, because her hour is come: but when she is delivered of the child, she remembereth no more the anguish, for the joy that a man is born into the world. And ye therefore now have sorrow: but I will see you again, and your heart shall rejoice, and your joy no one taketh away from you."
—St. John xvi. 21, 22.

On the score of taste, this sort of metaphor or illustration would scarcely suit the polite literature of the West at the present day; but no objection would be taken to it in the East. There is really no indelicacy about it; and it is admirably expressive of a time of pain and sorrow breaking forth into a lively joy.

The illustration rests on the Divine sentence regarding woman in childbirth recorded in the third chapter of Genesis, and it is used as a figure of things moral and spiritual in several books of the Old Testament. It therefore

came naturally into our Saviour's post-com-
munion . address to His disciples after the
mention of the vine, also a familiar symbol
or emblem in the Hebrew Scriptures.

The sentence pronounced on woman because
of the first transgression was that in sorrow
she should bring forth children. The Divine
words, in the very act of announcing travail,
suggested deliverance and joy ; for woman is
saved, and we all are saved "through the
child-bearing." * The offspring of woman
bruises the serpent's head. A recollection of
the promise to this effect perhaps accounts
for the marked and sympathetic manner in
which the Old Testament alludes to the
trouble and peril through which mothers
pass.† Not only so. It has led to personi-
fication of Zion or Jerusalem by the inspired
poets and prophets as a mother whose time
of tribulation would result in the multiplication of her children. Thus in one chapter of
Isaiah,‡ the Jewish nation suffering, yet not

* 1 Tim. ii. 15.

† We refer to the mention made of Rebekah, Rachel, and
the wife of the unworthy priest Phinehas.

‡ Isaiah xxvi. 17, 18.

profiting by affliction or yielding any adequate service to God, is likened to a woman who travails for an abortive birth. In another chapter of the same prophet,* the sudden prosperity of Zion is described as a joyful childbirth with little antecedent pain. "As soon as she travailed, she brought forth children." †

Both the prophet Isaiah and the Apostle Paul employ this domestic figure to illustrate their own anxiety under the burden of sacred ministry with which they were severally charged. The former, under a pre-vision of the capture of Babylon by the Medes and Persians, was acutely distressed. "Pangs have taken hold upon me, as the pangs of a woman that travaileth." ‡ The latter, full of solicitude for the Christian stability of the converts in Galatia, addressed them as his "little children, of whom I am again in travail until Christ be formed in

---

* Isaiah lxvi. 7, 8.

† Similar applications of the metaphor occur in Hosea xiii. and Micah iv. St. Paul has it as an illustration of sudden anguish in 1 Thess. v.

‡ Isaiah xxi. 3, 4.

you." * Indeed, St. Paul, though personally so free from family ties, seems to have been peculiarly alive to household feelings and affections. He described himself as a father with children in the gospel, many of them "begotten in his bonds;" as a mother yearning for the new birth of those to whom he ministered the Word; and as "a nurse cherishing her children," in his gentle care of the Church of God.

In one of the chief works of the same apostle occurs a famous passage representing the whole creation as travailing in pain while it waits for the resurrection of the saints. The earth is burdened, and its burden grows heavier; the sighs of creation are deep, and become deeper and more intense as the days go on. Nay, the Christians living on the earth groan within themselves; not indeed in despair, but in eager hope. All that expectation is a sort of travail; and the birth-throes will ultimately bring forth a joyful issue in the liberty of the glory of the sons of God.†

* Gal. iv. 19.   † Rom. viii. 19–25.

So much on the frequent use of this metaphor in Holy Writ. Now consider the particular use of it made by our Saviour. He had His profound trouble of soul, and was about to be "exceeding sorrowful, even unto death." * Isaiah had foretold this as being "the travail of His soul." But out of this issued His triumph and His glory. His reappearance from the grave was by a kind of new birth from a dark and silent womb. His first birth was from the virgin womb of Joseph's betrothed wife; His second from the virgin womb of another Joseph's sepulchre.

With His mind full of this travail and deliverance in the immediate future, Jesus employed the same illustration to cheer His desponding disciples. The deepening sorrow which hung upon them as His last sufferings drew near was the travail of their souls. Their Master felt for them. It is indeed most touching to see what consideration the Man of Sorrows had for their feelings, and how He provided consolation for them when a less perfect sufferer would have been engrossed

* St. John xii. 27 ; St. Matt. xxvi. 37, 38.

with his own imminent peril and his own
claim for sympathy. He felt their sorrow as
an accompanying shadow of His own ; and
He wished them to share the good hope which
dwelt within His breast. It was "for the joy
set before Him" that He "endured the cross,
despising the shame." He knew that because
of this travail of His soul He would be satisfied. He knew that His suffering would not
only precede, but also procure and produce
His glory. So He wished to lift His depressed
and anxious disciples into a participation of
this great comfort of hope. If they suffered
with Him, as "companions of His tribulation,"
they would also have their part in the joy
which was soon to be born out of all this
sorrow. He was to rise from the dead ; and
they were to see Him again as "a man born
into the world" from the very womb of
Hades.

And it was so. Though the eleven apostles
were not able at the time to enter into the full
consolation of their Master's words, and were
on that night and the two following days
quite overwhelmed with grief and conster-

nation at the capture, condemnation, and public crucifixion of their Lord, on the third day something occurred which made them forget their sorrow. That their travail continued up to the very morning of the resurrection is shown by the words of St. Mark, that Mary Magdalene "went and told them that had been with Him, as they mourned and wept." * But the fourth Gospel tells us that when Jesus reappeared among them "the disciples were glad when they saw the Lord." † Thereafter we find no trace of grief, or even of misgiving. Though the Lord departed from them into heaven, the apostles "returned to Jerusalem with great joy." ‡

But again there is travail. In each generation the Church of God has throes and inward pantings of desire and hope that the world does not understand. She is yearning to bring forth her children as children of God, born "of water and of the Spirit," and with Jesus Christ "formed in them." Alas! there is too little of this sacred travail. If there were

* St. Mark xvi. 10.　　　† St. John xx. 20.
‡ St. Luke xxiv. 52.

more, there would be more children. When the Church grows light-hearted and vainglorious, occupied (if one may so speak) with her dresses and her appearance, with her riches and honours, she is "barren and unfruitful." But when she has serious concern about spiritual life and its increase ; when she has prayerful throes and "groanings that cannot be uttered," these prove to be parturient pangs that are never in vain, but are rewarded by the birth of children who are to be heirs of God and joint-heirs with Christ.

Indeed, one may say that in the individual conscience and heart there are such pangs before it is safe or ordinarily possible to have the joy of salvation. They are good symptoms, those convictions of sin, throes of grief, and pantings of a burdened spirit. They precede and prepare for a new birth and a new life accompanied by a joy not easily blighted or snatched away. No doubt many men dread such inward pain, and think themselves well off because they have never had any religious anxiety, but have taken spiritual things coolly and been content to hope for the best. They too may have a kind of joy; but what a poor shallow thing it is compared with joy in the Lord! It is a matter of temperament, depends on "a good flow of spirits," swells with a temporary success, falls with every disappointment and defeat. Who can say of such joy, "No one can snatch it from me?" In truth, there is no way but through sorrow to imperishable joy.

In some respects the state of the disciples between the decease of their Master and His reappearance among them illustrates the anxiety of the Church during all the prolonged interval between His departure to the Father and His second coming. Obviously there are important points of difference. The disciples thought of Jesus as cut off by a cruel and shameful death, whereas the Church knows that He is living at the right hand of the Majesty on high. The disciples had the promise of the Comforter, whereas the Church has the presence of the Comforter. Still this great analogy holds good. The disciples waited, and the Church is waiting for the fulness of joy. They were encouraged to

expect the Saviour out of the realm of the
dead; the Church expects Him from the
heaven of heavens. The disciples were to
have their joy in the regeneration or resurrection of Him who was the Son of God; the
Church is to have her joy in the sublime regeneration or resurrection of the saints and
the manifestation of the sons of God.

O bright day when the Church shall see
her Lord in glory and be with Him—with
Him for ever! All preceding anguish will
be forgotten in that joy; all tribulation in
the glory which is to be revealed. Then
they that laugh now shall mourn and weep;
but they that weep now shall laugh. The
travail ends, and ends well.

XXXVI.

THE GREEN TREE AND THE DRY.

"For if they do these things in the green tree, what shall be done in the dry?"—St. Luke xxiii. 31.

IT relieves the brutal cruelty of the scene to read that "women bewailed and lamented" our Lord as He was led forth to be crucified. Of course, they were not interspersed with men in the crowd, as they are on occasions of popular excitement in our streets. According to Oriental usage, they must have been grouped by themselves; and from such a group rose a cry of grief and pity as the Just One, guarded by Roman soldiers and followed by Simon the Cyrenian carrying the cross, moved on to Calvary. Women in all future time and all countries have a right to reflect with pleasure that there is no mention in the Gospels of any woman rejecting Christ, or speaking to Him an unkind or disrespectful word.

The lamentation of the women did what all the mockery of the men could not do. It caused the Lord Jesus to break that sublime silence in which He was "enduring all things;" for He turned to them and warned them of the woe that was to come on their guilty city in their own days, or those of their children. His mind had been profoundly occupied with the impending doom of Jerusalem; and this, His last utterance before He was crucified, was a solemn and pathetic prophecy of its woful fall.

He ended it with a figurative or metaphorical saying. Every one knows the difference between green wood unfit to burn, and dry wood ready for the fire. But there has been divergence of opinion about the exact meaning or application of the figure on this particular occasion. Many have referred "the green tree" to Christ Himself, who deserved not to die, and "the dry tree" to the lifeless

and fruitless condition of Israel, deserving the
doom, and fit only for the doom, of a fiery
punishment. With this interpretation we
cannot feel satisfied. It is not likely that
the Saviour would describe His own innocence
by the phrase " the green tree," or that there
is an entire change of subject between the first
clause of the sentence and the second. Our
view is that the wood in both clauses has the
same reference. At first it is in a green or
moist state, but in time it becomes dry and
fit to be burned. The contrast then is not
between innocence and wickedness, but between wickedness immature and. wickedness
mature; and so the reference, all through,
is to the state of Jerusalem. It was the fig-
tree green, and putting forth leaves; but
soon it was to wither "from the root upwards," so that no more fruit could be
gathered from that dry tree; then it would
be fit only for the burning. So the Lord's
words may be paraphrased : "If this deed
of unjust violence, which draws forth your
cry of sorrow, O daughters of Jerusalem,

be done in this time of Israel's abundant leafage or show of godliness, what crimes shall be perpetrated in this city, and what judgment shall fall on it, when the iniquity is full and the patience of Heaven is exhausted?"

Jesus Christ was not so absorbed in His own sorrow as to be oblivious of the sorrow of others. Everywhere and always He had a Saviour's heart that yearned over the perishing. And as the shouts of the people moved Him to tears when He rode into the city, looked on it, and foresaw its ruin, so again the wailing cry of women stirred in Him thoughts of pity for the misery which women and children would endure in the horrors of the Roman siege. He had given to His disciples signs by which they might discern the approach of the great catastrophe and escape it; but those tender-hearted women! what a future lay before them and their children!

It is a warning of continually recurring application. It seems to many a light thing to reject Christ. No stroke from heaven falls upon them. The green tree is not consumed. But punishment delayed is not punishment escaped. When the iniquity is full, and the time for repentance spent, the green wood becomes dry; then follows the judgment of eternal fire.

INDEX.

PASSAGES OF SCRIPTURE TREATED OF.

By the same Author.

SYNOPTICAL LECTURES ON THE BOOKS OF
HOLY SCRIPTURE.

3 vols. 15s. Third Edition.

JAMES NISBET & CO.

(*A new Edition in preparation.*)

THE SPEECHES OF THE HOLY APOSTLES

(*Household Library of Exposition.*)

Second Edition, 3s. 6d.

HODDER & STOUGHTON.

THOMAS CHALMERS, D.D., LL.D.

(*Men Worth Remembering*).

2s. 6d.

HODDER & STOUGHTON.